THE TIMESHIFT

THE TIMESHIFT

can you change the hands of time?

MICHAEL T. GRACEY

Tate Publishing & *Enterprises*

Published by Tate Publishing & Enterprises, LLC
127 E. Trade Center Terrace | Mustang, Oklahoma 73064 USA
1.888.361.9473 | www.tatepublishing.com

Tate Publishing is committed to excellence in the publishing industry. The company reflects the philosophy established by the founders, based on Psalm 68:11,
"The Lord gave the word and great was the company of those who published it."

Cover design by Kandi Evans
Interior design by Jeff Fisher

Published in the United States of America

ISBN: 978-1-61566-016-2
1. Fiction, Science Fiction, General
2. Fiction, Action & Adventure
09.08.18

ACKNOWLEDGMENTS

I appreciate and want to thank LeTesia Callahan, Carolyn Chelette, Debbie Kemphart, and my dear wife, Beverly, who contributed and inspired the writing of this book.

CHAPTER 1

Only one block from Jim's house was the car of his dreams, a 1934 Plymouth coupe. His birthday was coming soon, but he had been assured that he was too young for a car. Jim confided in his friend Lloyd that he planned to buy the car anyway as they talked in the little shop behind Lloyd's house. Lloyd finally convinced Jim to wait until after his fourteenth birthday, on April 25, 1956, because Lloyd knew something that Jim did not know.

It was a sad April day at Woodrow Wilson Junior High, and when it ended, Don Downs's comments as Jim and Don walked out of the school together did not help matters.

"Look at the little black coupe," Don said. Jim looked up, and there was a 1934 Plymouth. Jim recognized it because he had been longing for that car, and now his brother-in-law, Ben Watson, was sitting in it. Ben had bought it for Jim. Jim could not describe the feeling as he drove his first car for the first time.

It was Jim's birthday, and he had the car he wanted to run the roads and drive to work at Rettig's Ice Cream Parlor on Proctor Street. The job was near the school, and the work times included after school until eleven p.m., weekends, and days during the summer months, but Jim did not let work interfere with working on his car. By the time summer arrived, the car's fenders were removed, and it took on the hot rod look Jim was after. Many times he would allow fifteen minutes to shower and get to work, then scrub the remaining grease from his hands after arriving at the ice-cream parlor.

On more than one occasion, the boys would pile into the hot rod coupe and head toward Hildebrandt Bayou to use the large bridge as a diving board. It was about thirty feet to the water, and most of the gang was willing to dive off it as if they were in a swimming pool. Jim would jump from the bridge, but diving into that murky water did not seem smart. The old car still had bald tires and didn't have a spare, so the twenty-mile trip was even more exciting thinking that they would be afoot at any time.

There were great times at Rettig's, but the money was not enough to buy all the things Jim wanted for his coupe. The easiest way to get things like tires, hub-caps, batteries, and parts was to steal them. Often he and some of the boys would ride around late at night after work and "lift" tires from cars parked along the street. Ray Robin once came up with four tires that he took from a Sears store after they had closed. He sold them to Lloyd for his Model A Ford Roadster for some extra cash. Jim's and Don's cars soon had large whitewall tires, and Jim had his rims reversed and painted red. That is when the boys decided to go into business for themselves. Along with the thrill of taking things and the feeling they were getting something for nothing, it provided lots of fun.

Don had a 1950 Chevy that was better than the 1934 Plymouth coupe due to the fact that his parents had money, where Jim had to work for his spending cash. There was one consolation when the boys raced: the coupe had the advantage of weight and Jim as driver. To prove the driving superiority, Don and Jim raced two 1950 Chevrolet cars one night behind the old high school, which was a great place to race. Don was driving his 1950 Chevy, and Jim was driving a 1950 Chevy that belonged to Don's dad. The boys raced, and Jim won. Jim drove the other 1950 Chevy and Don his dad's 1950 Chevy, and Jim won.

The stealing probably started when Jim and his friend Dennis were in the sixth grade. They went riding at night on their bicycles, kicking over garbage cans just for fun. One time they had ridden all the way to downtown Port Arthur, and they stopped at Walgreen's drug store for refreshment before riding back home. When Dennis walked out of the store, he showed Jim a bottle of wine he had lifted while they were inside. There was a great excitement about getting stuff without paying, and it was not long before Jim could get away with about anything small enough to slip under a shirt or coat. Over the next few months, the stealing became bolder, and the little group that rode to DeQueen Elementary School together joined the little shoplifting gang as they graduated to bigger things. They begin to take things from parked cars along the streets where they rode their bicycles and stole hubcaps for their older friends, like Lloyd and some of his buddies. Finally the keys in the ignition of a car could not be resisted. Jim and Ray Robin skipped school one day and found themselves near the old Thomas Jefferson High School tennis courts. They were already having a great time playing hooky, but one of them spied the keys in a telephone company repair truck, and they could see the workman was occupied up the utility pole. They jumped in the truck with Jim driving and laughed wildly as they rode around the neighborhood. Blasting along Thomas Boulevard, another telephone truck passed them heading in the other direction, and Jim waved to the workman as if he and Ray were on official business.

After ditching the truck near another school, Jim and Ray took a motor scooter from the parking area and headed out for more wild fun. When Jim stopped for a red light, a car full of boys pulled up behind them and piled out of the car. Jim saw what was about to happen and told Ray to run for it. Jim ran like a jackrabbit, but Ray was not fast enough to get away from the pursuers. Later, Ray related how he had been caught, beaten, and taken for a little ride by the outraged boys. The owner of the scooter had seen the theft and had jumped out of a classroom window, but how he got a group together and into a car was never explained.

The taking of other people's property had progressed beyond tires and parts for their cars. Jim still had a paper route that took him out at night to collect for the news and out early on Sunday mornings before anyone else was awake. Stealing was fairly easy because cars and trucks were not always locked, and some owners left their car keys in the car while parked in their own driveways. Lloyd was fascinated by the adventures of Jim and his gang and wanted to see how they did it. Late one night, Jim drove around with

Lloyd and Don until they spied a 1951 Chevy that was parked in a driveway in Griffin Park. Jim told Lloyd to wait around the corner as he eased out of the customized 1950 Studebaker. With a pair of alligator clips on a piece of wire, Jim connected two terminals on the ignition switch, and with another wire, he touched two other terminals to start the engine of the Chevy. He backed out into the street carefully and drove around the corner where Lloyd and Don waited. He told them, "Follow me," and then Jim drove the stolen car to the Proctor Street Extension and then off onto a dirt road, which put them out of town and in a dark, secluded area. Jim and Don started to strip anything from the car that could be used or sold. Lloyd became very nervous and was in a hurry to get away from the stolen car. He was older than the other boys and was smart enough to never again go with the boys or be involved in the operation. Lloyd did not want to be involved in any more stealing but had stolen whitewall tires on his roadster, an outboard motor, and an acetylene torch setup in his workshop that Jim had given him. The outboard motor was conveniently lying in the back of a pick-up truck that was parked a couple of blocks from the neighborhood and was used once by the boys on a rented boat to cruise on the Louisiana bayous. The acetylene torch was taken from the old high school late one night, and Lloyd used it to build his Model A Ford roadster. Another break-in at the high school cafeteria yielded boxes of candy, including the delicious Mars bars that had almonds in them. The excitement of stealing grew as the boys' bravery increased.

By the time the boys had finished the eighth grade, there was little they had not stolen, until something happened that changed the whole pattern. Jim had been contracted to supply a certain type of hubcap for an older boy in the neighborhood, and he had located a set on a car parked near the Gates Memorial Library. He skillfully removed the hubcaps from the parked car and placed them into the trunk of his mother's green 1950 Plymouth. He proceeded into the library to do a little school homework. When Jim had finished in the library, he returned to where the Plymouth had been parked and found that it was gone. *How ironic can you get?* Jim thought. He called the police from the library and explained that his car had been stolen, not knowing that a man had seen him stealing the hubcaps and had reported it to the police. A police car came to get Jim and took him to the police station for what turned out to be a setup.

The police decided to make a deal with Jim, which sounded like the only thing to do. Most of the group's activity had been around the homes of Jim and his friends, so they had been under suspicion for some time. This was their chance to come clean, and Jim agreed to convince his friends to turn themselves in with the promise that there would be only one charge against them for all of their activities. The police kept their promise about the charges but laughed their heads off at the stories the boys told of their escapades. All of the articles any of the boys still had were brought to the police station, excluding the things that were sold or could not be recovered. The boys were very serious through the confessions because they knew there could be big trouble for them, and it probably added to the officer's delight. The boys went to trial on a single charge of theft and got off with probation, which they all thought was very light punishment. All of the boys involved came to an agreement that they would never get mixed up in a deal like that again and would stop their taking ways.

Even though Jim was the leader of the group, some of them got together and decided that it had been Jim's fault they had been caught. They decided to give Jim the cold treatment, and that is the way the group ended their association for the time being.

Jim decided that his best friends were gone and that he would visit his brother in Ohio, as his mother had suggested sometime earlier. The 1956–57 school years had already started when Jim boarded a bus for Hamilton, Ohio, and left his 1934 Plymouth in the old garage behind his mother's house on Eleventh Street.

Jim's brother Louie came to the bus station to get him upon arrival in Hamilton for the first time. He had a house on Buckeye Street about ten blocks from Roosevelt Junior High School where Jim was to attend his ninth-grade year. Classes had been in session for a few weeks, so the new kid from Texas caused quite a stir around school. Jim was six feet tall and about 160 pounds with blond hair and blue eyes. His hair was styled after the late movie star James Dean, and he had a red nylon jacket to go with the look. Most everyone was friendly, and Jim was invited to enter into sports by the coach as soon as he heard that he had played football, run track, and played basketball. The football season was about over, and the first Friday night at the new school, a group of boys asked Jim to go with them to the football game. It was the first time Jim had ever gone to school with Negroes, but he tried to be polite to everyone, and soon all of the school knew him as Tex. The boys at the football game told Jim of some of their exploits like lifting and sitting a Volkswagen on the back porch of a house one night. Jim wanted friends, but he was not about to get into trouble with a new group of boys in Hamilton. It began to snow, which was a thrill for Jim, being from warm Port Arthur, so he decided it was time to head home. The boys pointed him in the right direction, but, being so new in the area, it was not long before Jim was lost. He walked down unfamiliar streets until he could tell that he was in the black part of town. Someone yelled out "Hey, Tex, what you doing in this neighborhood?" Jim was glad to see some of the guys from gym class and to get new directions for the walk to Buckeye Street.

There was a girl named Barbara Holt who seemed very interesting and indicated to Jim that she would like to get together. Barbara was one of the most popular girls in school and was petite with a beautiful face and great shape. She showed him where she lived one afternoon after school, and they started getting friendlier and soon began to date. Jim's brother agreed to let him drive the family car on a very limited basis, and dating was one of the ways to get the 1954 Nash Ambassador on a Saturday night. One of the first dates that Jim and Barbara made was to the new Elvis movie, *Love Me Tender,* at the movie theater on the town square of Hamilton. They were very cozy in the dark movie, but as they left the theater, an older boy made some comments about Jim and Barbara. She explained on the way home that she had broken up with Butch some time ago, and he was still trying to get back together. Butch had a cool 1949 Chevy with loud dual exhaust, and he had dropped out of school to work as a mechanic.

Jim walked a lot around Hamilton because he

did not have a car and the other boys in his class did not have a driver's licenses. One night Jim was cutting through a field near the school when Butch and a few of his friends stopped him for a confrontation. Butch said he wanted to fight and was very surprised when Jim said to him, "I don't really want to fight, but if you are not willing to talk about what is bothering you, let's get it on." Jim started taking off his coat when Butch had a change of mind. He agreed to talk about it and told Jim, "I don't like you dating my girlfriend, Barbara." Jim assured him that as long as Barbara wanted to date him, Butch should leave her alone until she got over it. He convinced Butch that acting bad was not going to get her back, so Jim continued to date Barbara until they had an argument about her seeing Butch. Jim heard that Barbara had gone for a ride with Butch, so he confronted her by saying, "Why would you go out with Butch after all you have told me about him?"

"I can go out with anyone I please," she said, which was not what Jim wanted to hear. He started giving her the cold shoulder, and it made her very upset with Jim. Being the kid from Texas, it did not take long before Jim was seeing Cheryl, a pretty blonde girl who was more ladylike than Barbara. It turned out that Cheryl's parents were absolutely against car dates until she was eighteen years old, so they met at the movies and after school because they liked each other. Jim could go to her house under her mother's supervision, but when it came time for the ninth grade graduation dance, the car date rule was set in stone.

Jim played basketball when the season came, so there were games and road trips that were fun for him. Being around the black guys was usually fine, and they liked to call him Tex and kid around with each other. One time Jim said the wrong thing during one of the locker-room kidding sessions, and one of the biggest black boys on the team wanted to fight that day after school. During the shower session after a hard basketball practice, Jim said, "Hey, Dave, you know that color will not wash off."

"We gonna have to meet behind the gym after school to settle this, Tex."

As usual, Jim showed up for any challenge. The black boys were well represented, and a few of Jim's white friends were there too. Jim would never back down but had a way of defusing most situations by saying, "I am sorry that you took it personally, but I did not mean anything by it. I was kidding like everyone does, but if you want to fight about it, let's get to it." Somehow the anger was past by that time, and the tall black player did not want to test Jim's skills as a fighter. One reason Jim did not have to fight much was that he would usually pick the biggest, meanest boy and make sure that everyone knew he could whip that guy. John was as strong and tough as anyone at Roosevelt, so when it came time for boxing as part of gym classes, he was paired with Jim. John came at Jim determined to do damage, and Jim dodged and weaved until John caught him with a punch that broke John's thumb. The fight was over, and all the gym boys knew was that Tex had whipped John as far as they were concerned.

There was also an attitude that Jim would exhibit that let the other boys know that he would not back down, *so don't push unless you are ready to fight.* Walking down the hall one day, a really tall boy stopped Jim and said, "When I first saw you, I knew that we would fight, but I see you are friendly and I would like to be friends." He and Jim became good friends while he was at Roosevelt Junior High School.

A boy named Gordon Warren lived one block from the house on Buckeye, and Jim would see him at school or in the neighborhood sometimes. He had an older sister named Mabel and an older brother with a white 1956 Buick convertible that sat outside all the time. The white paint was dirty, and the top needed cleaning. The older brother also had an airplane, of all things. After Jim became friends with this family from Kentucky (called briar hoppers), Jim would visit and talk with Mr. Warren about Texas while he would relate stories of coon hunting in Kentucky. The derogatory term "briar hoppers" are people from the backwoods of the mountainous state of Kentucky and were open and kind folks. The older brother did not mind if Jim drove the Buick, so Jim suggested that he and Gordon wash it and clean the top and inside for his brother. The car turned out to be a beauty and ran like a scaled dog. Jim was not familiar with the hills and wooded highways, but driving in that part of the country was a pleasure for him. They could put the top down and take his friends from school out for a ride from time to time. One night someone yelled, "Stop the car!" and they jumped out on a lonely road to grab a large mailbox. Jim did not like it, but they took it to the school and left it on a windowsill. Everyone had a big laugh, even though Jim did not want to get into any trouble.

Jim enjoyed the time in Hamilton and had his first real pizza when Mabel took him to a takeout place; they ate the hot pizza in the car. It was great, probably the best he would ever have. Louie got Jim a job at the

Green Lantern Bar outside of Hamilton when Richard Solozo decided to open a pizza place in one corner of the bar room. Jim would make his way to work after school to cut pepperoni, grate cheese, and prepare the other ingredients just the way Dick Solozo had showed him. By the time the bar crowd showed up and took their usual places, it was time for Jim to head home. Louie worked as a bartender as a side job to his Civil Defense Recruiting job that he did for the US Air Force.

Jim was supposed to catch the bus to go to work, but it cost money. He did not like to wait on a corner for a bus, so he would often run all the way to work along the Erie Highway that passed through Hamilton. Sometimes he would get a ride home with Louie or catch the bus. The money began to roll in, and Jim would carry a hundred or two in his billfold, but when Louie found out, he convinced Jim that it was unsafe to carry money like that. He suggested that he would save the money for Jim so he could have it when he went back to Port Arthur.

The end of the school year was getting near when Louie was to be transferred to another place with his air force job. The Warren family invited Jim to stay with them until school was out, and then he could join Louie at the Freish farm in Michigan, where Louie and his family would be staying for the summer. That worked well because Jim could help get Gordon out of bed for school and use the Buick just about any time. Old Mr. Warren would say at the dinner table every night, "We are waiting on you, just like one hound dog waits on another," but Mr. and Mrs. Warren were fine Kentucky people, and Jim felt at home in the large house on Buckeye.

Gordon liked the boots that Jim wore and the western hat that he would wear on occasion. He also purchased boots and a hat to wear to school so he could be like Tex. It was Jim's brother Louie who first started calling him "Cowboy." The name stuck, so his nickname became Cowboy, and that made Gordon very happy.

Cheryl's parents would not let Jim take her to the ninth grade dance, so they met there and enjoyed the school party. Part of the activities included voting for the most popular boy and girl of the ninth grade class. Jim should have been voted in as most popular boy, but, having been there less than a year, another boy was chosen to be with Barbara Holt on stage. Jim did receive a school letter in basketball and track, plus he left a school record for the broad jump, which stood for many years.

It was time for Jim to leave Hamilton, and the plan was to take the Greyhound bus to Cold Water, Michigan, to meet Louie. Gordon's brother came up with an alternate plan, so instead of buying a bus ticket, Jim gave the brother the money for a ride to Michigan in his airplane. The trip went well, and they landed at the Cold Water airport, where Louie's wife came to get Jim.

Louie had married a girl from Michigan while they were both in the air force. She was hard to be around, but Louie had three children by then, and there was no way he would leave them with their mother. When he arrived at the one hundred-acre farm off the main highway, it was Jim's first time to stay on a farm (except for one trip to Ragley, Louisiana, with a friend when they were younger), so he was very excited to see how a farm operated. Mr. and Mrs.

Friesh purchased the farm to raise crops and sell milk from their dairy cows. During the time he was there, Louie attempted to take him fishing and act like an older brother should. When it was time for Louie and his family to report to his next duty location, Jim stayed at the farm and helped as much as possible to earn his keep. Up before daybreak, Mrs. Freish would have breakfast for Jim, and then he would start work for the day. There was a 1930 Chevrolet flatbed truck that could be used to receive the hard corn ears that Jim twisted from the shucks and threw into the old truck. He worked until lunchtime picking corn and then headed to the house for a home-cooked meal. After lunch, there was usually some assignment that kept Jim busy the rest of the day. One night, some of the relatives that lived next door asked if Jim wanted to spear fish with them, and it sounded like fun. There was a gas flame over the front of the boat, so the fish in the clear stream water could be seen well enough to spear them for tomorrow's supper. The work and adventures lasted all summer, and then Louie came back with his family for the trip back to Port Arthur. Any trip with that family was a nightmare, but they arrived back in Port Arthur in June 1957.

CHAPTER 2

Don and Jim had written a few times over the last school year and had exchanged a book named "Street Rod," about a boy with a hot rod coupe, a start to re-establishing a friendship that was broken by the trouble with the law in Port Arthur. Jim called Don to let him know that he had arrived back in Port Arthur, and Don came over immediately in his newest car, a 1951 baby blue Ford two-door sedan. They went for a ride to downtown Port Arthur and parked in front of a store where Don had to get something for his mom. The Ford was lowered all the way around and had a flat-head V-8 with a good set of pipes. The passenger's seat went too far back, so a little piece of wood had to be placed between the seat and the vertical stop. Jim leaned too far back on the ride to town, and then Don told him about the fix. The boys cautiously became friendly and told each other more about what had been going on in their lives.

The 1934 Plymouth was sold to a couple of guys for fifty dollars, and they came to pull the car out of the garage. With the money that Jim had been saving and the sale of the '34 Plymouth coupe, he began to search for the right car in which to begin Thomas Jefferson High School. During the time in Ohio, Jim had looked at many cars and decided a 1950 Ford or Chevrolet would be a good choice. He drove several cars in Port Arthur, Beaumont, and the surrounding area, but none of them seemed right. It was a rainy day when Jim found the car he had been looking for, and he hurried home to tell his mom all about it. He persuaded his mom to go back with him to the Lynn Ford used car lot near downtown Port Arthur for a ride in it while convincing her to help him buy it. She came up with a better idea than Jim had hoped for when she offered to buy the car for $295 and let Jim use his money to fix it up. It was a 1950 Mercury coupe two-door with flathead V-8 engine and overdrive. The salesman said that the car was owned by a little old lady, and Jim believed him because the inside of the car was like new, but the outside showed its seven-year age. It was exactly what Jim had in mind, and it drove like a dream when he headed down Proctor Street toward the house on Eleventh Street in a misty rain. He parked his latest love in the driveway near the street as the rain started in earnest. The radio newscast told about a hurricane heading for the Texas coast that would arrive about nine o'clock in the morning of the next day. At daybreak, Jim was at the front window of the house in his dad's old chair watching the 1950 Mercury as if he could protect it somehow. On that day June 27, 1957, Hurricane Audrey rolled over the car, the house, and the yard of the house on Eleventh Street, while only three miles away in Cameron, Louisiana, hundreds of people lost their lives to 145-mile-per-hour hurricane-force winds, high water, and snakebites. Being only fifteen years old and having no dad to go with him, Jim was not part of the Port Arthur group that went to Cameron to help with disaster relief. The high water and tropical storms were not unusual in Port Arthur summer months, so Jim went about cleaning up his Merc and enjoying the finest automobile he had ever owned. It was much later when Jim read that Hurricane Audrey was the first named storm and was the first storm to reach Category 4 status. It was a powerful hurricane that left $1 billion in damage and took at least 419 lives. The name Audrey was retired and would never be used again to label a hurricane.

In the weeks that followed, the car took on a different appearance because it was lowered within a few inches of the street and had a new shiny black paint job. Whitewall tires with flipper hubcaps were also added to the car to align it with the best customizing taste of the day. Pinstripes and pipes were added to complete the transformation from a little old lady's car to a beautiful "Let's make the drag" car. The drag in Port Arthur had been the thing for kids to do as long as Jim could remember. His sisters and their boyfriends would make the drag, and sometimes Jim would be allowed to go along with them. On Friday night and Saturday night every kid in town wanted to be on Proctor Street to make a circuit that included some of the drive-in restaurants. They were there to see and be seen, but it was even more fun if a kid had a really cool car. Cruising down Proctor, stopping at red lights, hitting the drive-ins, and maybe having a little race made for a great night. If the race challenge was serious, it could be taken to Rubber Plant Road, which was a stretch of highway that had been marked for drag racing by the local kids.

Jim got a good job in a nearby community at a Sinclair service station in Groves, Texas, through a friend. During slack hours, he could work on his Merc and get ready for the occasional races on Rubber Plant Road or behind the old high school. Several boys from Groves who liked cars as much as Jim did would stop by the station to get gas or get service on their cars. Bill, Jerry, David, Frankie, and Jim started talking about how they needed a car club and should start one of their own. From the group discussions, the Night Hawk Custom Car Club was formed, and Jim was elected president of the organization. The town name was omitted from the official name of the club so that boys from Groves, Port Neches, and Port Arthur could all feel like it was not restricted to one city. Meetings were held at the Sinclair station on Monday nights, and afterward, the group would file out to the Rubber Plant Road to match their cars in a quarter-mile drag. Lookouts were posted because racing was illegal, but the road was a favorite place to drag because it was not used much in those days. Occasionally, a police car would come along and break up the racing; later the fuzz would patrol the road on a regular basis, which made it even more thrilling.

The new car club grew in membership with the addition of old friends like Gary, Larry, Don, and Greg, who all contributed greatly to running the organization. The treasury increased to a point where Bill suggested they have a first class party at his house in Groves. Most of the boys were around fifteen years old with a few older boys around seventeen. Bill was one of the older boys and had the philosophy of "Ride on Rubber. It's safer." No one ever knew what that meant, but it became the Night Hawk parting cry, and the parties soon became part of the club's philosophy. Bill and Jim made the preparations for the party and included all of the refreshments they could think to include. The table was set with chips, dips, olives, crackers, spreads, and a large punch bowl that somehow got spiked by the time Night Hawk boys and their dates arrived. The dip was made of Velveeta cheese and Rotel tomatoes that were melted together, which began another tradition at all Night Hawk parties. Everyone was in a party mood, and soon they were dancing in the dark living room of Bill's parents' house. The refreshments went fast, and the party began to slow down, which forced Bill to suggest they come up with some way to make things lively again. From a quick huddle in a corner, the boys decided to take the girls on a snipe hunt by leading them all to the middle of a golf course behind Bill's house, which was to serve as the traditional *woods* where unsuspecting victims were usually left holding the bag. All the detailed instructions were given to the girls about holding the bag while the boys herded the snipes to them. If the girls knew what was happening, they did not let the boys know. After the boys had a big laugh back at the house, Bill came up with an idea to scare the girls who were waiting out in the dark. He suggested that someone would wear a raincoat and get on his shoulders so they could build a large man to make a figure about nine feet tall. With their homemade monster, the boys went back to the golf course expecting to have some fun scaring the girls, but the girls jumped the tall figure, and they all joined in rolling around in the grass, laughing about the whole thing. Most of these girls became Night Hawk steady girlfriends, and the famous parties continued for the next three years.

Jim's dad, Louie Sr., had come to Port Arthur, Texas, in 1929 and began work at the Standard Brass for a man named Leblanc. The story was told many times about how he was walking down the beach on Bolivar Peninsula when he saw some guys building a beach cabin. He stopped to help, and they hired him to go to work at the owner's foundry in Port Arthur. Having a job, he went back to Shreveport, Louisiana, long enough to convince his childhood sweetheart to marry him and move to Port Arthur. Jim was the fourth child born to this family, and Louie Sr. worked hard to make a living in the foundry for twenty-eight years. He liked to stop at the places in downtown Port Arthur to have a few beers and play dominoes, so he was usually at one of the places with names like the Keyhole Club or Jones Smokehouse when Jim wanted to see him. Louie Sr. told Jim about the gambling that was common in those places and how the professional gamblers wore a red feather in their hats to let others know they weren't trying to hustle anyone. Jim's dad drank Budweiser beer and smoked Camel cigarettes; there was no such thing as light beer or filtered cigarettes in those days. The term "smokehouse" was a very good name for the clubs, and they smelled of stale beer and smoke. As far as Jim knew, Louie Sr. did not participate in any of the other pleasures of Port Arthur like the twenty-seven houses of prostitution in the immediate area. Jim's dad died in 1955, just before Jim became aware of the vice in Port Arthur, so they never discussed the subject. By 1957, Jim and his friends had cars, girlfriends, and could get booze any time they wanted. The fake ID was nothing new, and Jim had one that said he was twenty-seven years old with red hair, when he was fifteen years old and had blond hair. Two old ladies ran a liquor store on Houston Avenue and were always glad to see the tall young man with his polite attitude come into the store. When his friends were thirsty, Jim would go into the store with the money collected from the boys and buy the beer and one bag of potato chips. He usually only wanted one of the beers, and it took the salty potato chips to finish it. Along Houston Avenue were a couple of the whorehouses that Jim's friends wanted to visit, so he would go along with them to enjoy seeing the scantily dressed girls and hang out in the parlor, which was like a living room of a house in most cases. Marcella's on Seventh Street was one of the nicest whorehouses and had a front room that looked like a bar room instead of a living room. Beer was fifty cents a can, and the trip upstairs cost two dollars, which was a lot of money for most of the boys, except Don. The boys could buy a cold six-pack for one dollar, and the movies cost twenty-five cents in those days, but Don's parent were rich and gave him large sums of money at Christmas and birthdays. Don liked going with the girls more than any of his friends, and he began to know them personally. He told his buddies that some of them were married, and it was their way to make a living; it did not mean anything to them to *date* other men. Jim did not care to go with the whores because there was no passion or desire other than seeing them in their nighties or without clothes. The main reason that Jim would go with the boys to those places was because everything was closed in Port Arthur after eleven p.m., and it meant going home after a date or making the drag all night. One night while at Marcella's, the lady behind the bar shouted for everyone to leave immediately because the Texas Rangers were on their way. It dawned on Jim that the local police and officials were involved in the illegal activities of gambling, prostitution, and crime in Port Arthur, hence the name the Wicked City. Another place that Jim's friends liked was *Gracie's Wood Yard,* which was across the tracks in the black part of town. Just down the street from *Gracie's* was a black whorehouse, so Jim and Don had to visit there at least one time. It was a different experience to go to bed with a black girl.

In spite of all the temptations, Jim would rather have a nice girlfriend and drive his hot rod cars up and down the drag. The Night Hawks were a great bunch to party with and to have as friends. They all knew each other from the monthly meetings and controlled membership, while the outsiders knew them by their black jackets and club placket swinging from rear bumpers. The boys tried to help others on the street with flat tires or stalled engines so that the Night Hawks would be known for showing kindness to others. They had white coveralls with their emblem on the back and had business-type cards that would let others know who helped them.

Jim and many of the others graduated from Thomas Jefferson High School in 1960 and left the club to a younger group. Jim and Larry headed to college and both became engineers living away from ole Port Arthur. Shortly after their graduation from high school, the Texas Senate investigated the corruption in the Port Arthur city government, including the police department. The whorehouses were shut down, and the gambling was curtailed. The downtown area became like a ghost town when businesses closed and the black community moved into areas that were once reserved for whites only. The civil rights movement began to integrate Port Arthur, so the whites moved to Mid-County, Nederland, and Port Neches/Groves to get out of the Port Arthur jurisdiction. Property values went down in the Eleventh Street neighborhood when the Vietnamese were moved into the vacant houses, and Jim finally moved his mother to Houston in 1976 at her request. The old house on Eleventh Street sold for five thousand dollars but is still in use in today.

CHAPTER 3

In 1958 in the Gulf coast town of Port Arthur, summer had finally arrived after Jim's and Larry's first years in high school. Thomas Jefferson High School was the home of the Yellow Jackets football team and would later be famous for students such as Janis Joplin, a music icon, and Jimmy Johnson, a football coaching celebrity. Port Arthur is located in Jefferson County, which is southeast Texas. Founded by Arthur Stilwell in the late nineteenth century, it became the largest oil refinery network in the world. Port Arthur experienced an economic decline under the corrupt administration of Mayor J. P. "Pink" Logan, which inspired the clean government movement established by Logan's primary adversary, W. C. Welch. This effort ultimately led Dallas Representative Tom James to identify corruption and graft at all levels of the municipal government and law enforcement. The report did not end corruption but merely pushed all of the rackets into the underground. The kids of those times were not part of the corruption, and it only made living in Port Arthur more exciting for teenagers.

It was hard to believe that their mothers would consent to a weekend trip, but, of course, they would be staying with Jim's relatives in Shreveport, Louisiana. Friday came at last, and Larry was ready to go when Jim got off work from his summer job at a small hamburger stand called the Chuck Wagon. The boys hit the road in Larry's royal blue 1964 Mercury that was lowered and slicked in the fashion of the day. The overhead valve V-8 engine, standard shift, and custom look enhanced the enjoyment of rumbling along the highway while discussing the big plans they had for the weekend. They sang along with the radio and laughed about recent events, but heading two hundred miles away from home gave them a feeling of freedom they had not experienced before. Jim and Larry had girlfriends but had not had much experience with sex or women of the world. Port Arthur was a rather small town, and the boys were young. Boys did not talk about such things on a general basis and would not date anything but "good girls," as they were called in those days. They thought that maybe on the trip they would look for girls who were ready for love, so when they saw two girls walking along the road just outside Many, Louisiana, they stopped the car and drove back to them and said, "Hey, ah, ah ... How many miles to Many?" Needless to say, that did not impress the two girls. They were too flustered to ask anything else, so they quickly drove on toward the small town of Many. A later joke between the two boys was, "How many to Many?"

On his previous visit to Shreveport, Jim had learned about the nightclubs in Bossier City and had tasted his first Tom Collins. Neither of the boys knew much about drinking, but their plans were to have a good time no matter what.

It was about ten o'clock on Friday night when the boys arrived in Shreveport and decided to head straight for the Bossier City nightclub strip. They stopped at several of the clubs for a Tom Collins and a wide-eyed look around the glittering establishments. Finally, they arrived at a bar at the end of the strip where the band was playing country music. That type of club was too much for the rock-and-roll Port Arthur youths, so they decided to head back across the river to Shreveport. It wasn't long before they were in a part of town that was unfamiliar to Jim, but, feeling no concern, they drove around until they spied two girls sitting on the steps of a house. Taking a closer look, they discovered the girls had beer and were smoking. They must have been the girls they had been looking for, so Jim and Larry parked around the corner so they could walk slowly past the house. They did not realize how long the block was, so seeing that the car was far away, Jim decided to make his move. Walking up to the girls sitting on the porch of the old white house in the strange neighborhood, he said something meaningless, like, "How y'all doing?" Not to be left out of the good times, Larry soon joined the group, and the boys managed to get a conversation started. The boys were sixteen years old, and the two girls were much older than Jim and Larry, probably twenty years old, but they drank beer together and spent the night learning new songs from the girls.

"Here is number one, the fun has just begun, roll me over in the clover do it again. Roll me over in the clover; roll me over lay me down and do it again."

Another college song that they sang sounded like a fraternity song named Sigma Nu, and it had words like, "Never trust a Sigma Nu because they will screw you." The next morning the boys drove to the bus station in Shreveport and cleaned up the best they could before heading to Jim's cousin's house on Broadacres Road, acting like they had just arrived in town.

Saturday was spent visiting with Jim's relatives, and Larry got acquainted with Janis, who was Jim's cousin. Janis and Jim were the same age and had grown up together through family visits to Shreveport each year for the Louisiana State Fair and visits to Port Arthur for trips to the beach and fresh seafood. Jim started driving at an early age and had his license by age fourteen, so when he had last visited Shreveport, they were allowed to take the family car over to Bossier City for that first Tom Collins. All they had to do was walk into a club and order any drink they wanted; wow, what a place.

Janis was a brunette with sky blue eyes and the figure of a fashion model. She called a friend to come over to meet her cousin Jim, and he spent the rest of the day getting acquainted with Dianne, who had soft blonde hair, green eyes, and a full body. She took to Jim immediately as if he reminded her of someone, and he loved the romantic attention. The time finally came for the big Saturday night date, and the boys dressed in suits and the girls put on their nicest dresses. They all tingled with excitement as the blue Mercury headed toward Bossier City and the nightclub strip. In Jim's and Larry's minds, those places were unbelievable with their scantily dressed waitresses, low lights, and mixed drinks for the asking. It did not take long for the group to get high on the drinks and the atmosphere of each place they visited. After stopping at the best clubs, the little group wound up at the Twilight Club about eleven o'clock. By that time, Larry had become roaring drunk and started visiting other tables, giving them some form of philosophy, and finally collapsed on a coffee table in the lounge area and smashed it flat. Jim managed to get him out the back door and to the car and then quickly returned to the club to get the girls before someone saw the broken coffee table. On the way out with the girls, Jim's date passed out, so he held her up until they were safely to the car where Larry also lay passed out. It was discovered later that Larry had never had a drink before and just did not know how to handle it. It was also discovered that Dianne was carrying a torch (as it was termed in those days) for an old boyfriend named Wayne, because as soon as she recovered, she cried and called for Wayne until Janis and Jim had enough of it. Nothing they said or suggested stopped Dianne from continuing her cries for Wayne. With Jim driving, they made it to the local hangout where they found Wayne and turned Dianne over to him. Jim was glad to stop her crying but was sad to see her go because he had become fond of her. The three remaining dizzy and tired kids drove back to Janis's house on Broadacres Road so they could recover from the night of fun. The headaches and sick stomachs lasted into the next day. After the trouble with Dianne, a girl's old boyfriend was referred to as "a Wayne," and a few days later back in Port Arthur, Larry and Jim would meet another girl with "a Wayne."

By Sunday afternoon, the boys had recuperated, packed their bags, and were ready to leave for home, supposedly. The plan was to find their friend Lloyd, a buddy from home, who was stationed at Barksdale Air Force Base in Bossier City. By some stroke of luck, they were able to locate him, and Lloyd took the boys for a tour of the base. He told them that beer could be purchased for less on the base, so they loaded three cases in the trunk of Lloyd's car and carried two six packs of cold beer in the car with them. Of course, Jim had to have his potato chips to go with the beer. They decided to take a little ride around the area and have a beer, but the first beer had not been finished before they spotted five girls walking down the street in front of a drive-in movie near town. With nothing to lose but his virginity, Larry said, "Hey, y'all want a ride?" The girls hesitated for a minute and then agreed to climb in while uttering some profane remark that the boys could not quite make out. As the girl pick-ups got into the black Chevy coupe, the boys thought they had it made. Three of the girls sat in the back with Larry and Jim while the other two sat in the front seat with Lloyd. Everything was orderly for about two minutes after introductions, then with the opening of the beer, one of the girls spilled some on another girl and the brawl began. From all the cussing and yelling, the two weekend travelers just knew that the girls would do anything. They both tried to get Lloyd to drive to the country away from town, but before they had driven very far, one of the girls yelled, "Stop the car," and they all piled out. That was the last the boys saw of those girls, and all that was left of the refreshment were empty cans on the floor of Lloyd's car. Jim couldn't find a trace of the potato chips.

Back at the air base, the boys parted company with Lloyd at the gate where Larry's car was parked, and they agreed to meet him the next day for the trip to

Port Arthur. The boys took one more trip to the Bossier City strip for a last look and maybe a little drink. Sometime that night Larry said to Jim that he had something very important to tell him and that he had wanted to say it. Jim thought it was something really big and important, so he listened intently when Larry said, "You walk around with part of your handkerchief sticking out of your back pocket." Jim thought that it sounded ridiculous, but Larry was very serious and explained to Jim that it made him look like he did not care about anything. After the talk, Jim tried not to let his handkerchief show again since it meant so much to Larry.

The boys slept in the car on Sunday night but didn't know where because they were exhausted and still a little hungover. Monday morning they washed at the bus station again and wondered what to do all day while they waited for Lloyd to get off duty at the air base. Stopping in downtown Shreveport, they had breakfast at a little café and then walked around for a while, waiting for the movie house to open. Their walk took them near the bridge that spans the Red River between Shreveport and Bossier City and then back to the movie theater as they bided their time. Because of the excess drinking, the boys still felt elevated, especially when they drank water. Once in the theater, they chose seats behind two young couples. When the two boys left their dates to go to the lobby for popcorn, Jim and Larry surprised themselves by taking the vacant seats by the two girls. By the time their boyfriends returned from the lobby with the refreshments, Jim and Larry had become acquainted with the girls, and the two other guys had to take seats elsewhere. What luck! Two beautiful girls and Jim had the prettiest one.

Jim and Larry became as friendly as possible with the girls during the movie and persuaded them to accept a ride home after the show. A problem arose when they left the building; it was still daylight outside, and Jim and Larry had not made such a good bargain after all. Larry's girl was much too tall for him, and Jim's girl was not the beauty she had been in the dark. Not only were they rather homely, but they lived ten miles out of town. The boys dutifully delivered the two girls home safely and headed back toward Barksdale Air Force Base. The only good thing about meeting the girls and taking them home was that it killed enough time so that Lloyd was ready to head to Port Arthur. Larry and Jim, in the blue Mercury, followed Lloyd through town and to the highway leading toward the Texas line, stopping only long enough at a roadside park to have a cold beer.

Having arrived back in Port Arthur safely, Jim and Larry headed home to clean up for a visit to a new girlfriend that Larry had been keeping to himself. Her name was Gloria, and she was a petite, dark-haired girl who looked like a cheerleader. She had a friend over that afternoon, and they were making papier-mâché maps for a class at school. Jim had some artistic talent and soon became acquainted with Karen, who was Gloria's best friend. She was a tall, blue-eyed blonde and was as shapely as they come. The afternoon was pleasant and productive because by the time they finished the maps, Jim and Larry both had dates for the night. Excitedly, Jim and Larry headed home to get ready for their big night with the girls, and Jim drove his car for the double date to make the drag down Proctor Street. It was not long before Larry announced to Jim that there was a "Wayne," and he instantly knew what that meant. The problem was that Jim thought Larry meant that there was another Wayne in the picture for Karen. It turned out that Larry meant that Gloria had a Wayne in her recent past, and it would take some time for he and Gloria to get better acquainted. A girl who carried a torch for another guy in those days was a big obstacle.

CHAPTER 4

The weekend after Larry and Jim got home from the trip to Shreveport, they planned a beer party at the beach. Jim's black lowered machine was loaded with the iced-down brew, and the club cars headed out of town toward Sabine Pass and then on to McFadden beach, about twenty-five miles away. These beach parties were fairly common, especially in the summer when there was no school and time for such activities. New ideas were always welcome to improve the good time on the sandy beach. One time they tried to spike a watermelon with vodka, which did not turn out too well, but it was something different. The beach was a good place to take dates and enjoy a large fire of driftwood, roasted wieners, a picnic, and making out. That trip the club had the three cases of beer that were brought from Shreveport, and they agreed not to bring dates. The plan was to have a good beer-drinking time without having to get home early.

The custom cars arrived at McFadden Beach

around midday and eased off the highway and onto the sand. They passed the food joint called the Breeze Inn and began a search for good parking. They soon found the spot they were looking for next to some girls. Most of the day was spent chasing the girls on the hot sand and drinking the cold beer. Their endeavor was only interrupted by swims in the cool, salty gulf water. Larry had a quirk when he drank too much. If he was in the woods, he would run out of sight and return sometime much later. When at the beach, he would swim out of sight, and his friends thought that they would never see him again. In spite of the beer, the beach road, and Larry's long swim, they all made it home without serious injury.

A couple of months went by, and it became time to plan the next big Night Hawk event, so Jack Smith and Jim Gray discussed a weekend at Nibblets Bluff near Vinton, Louisiana. Jack's family had a nice cabin in the woods near the irrigation canal where the kids liked to go for outings. This time the plan called for leaving the dates at home and having a big blowout in a safe place where no one would have to drive home in a drunken condition. Nibblets Bluff included a water-lift pump station that discharged into a canal. The kids would sometimes drive the sixty-five miles there to have a picnic and go swimming. It was fun to jump into the powerful discharge of water and be swept down the canal for a couple hundred yards. All the details were discussed at the club meeting, and the famous "Jack's camp" weekend was approaching. Jim purchased the alcoholic beverages with his fake ID, as usual, and food was purchased with club funds for the big party that would start on Friday night. Jim, Larry, and Earl purposely made no dates so they could go on Friday, but many of the group said they had dates and could not come until late on Friday or early on Saturday. Even Jack was going to come in later, so Jim agreed to open the cabin and get ready for the party to start late on Friday night. All went well getting to the cabin and unloading the supplies, but as it got dark and the hours dragged by, the boys got into the beverages ... big time. Jim, Larry, and Earl started drinking the beer and then the whiskey so that by ten p.m., they were plastered. Larry disappeared outside. Jim and Earl were surprised when there came a knock on the door and two policemen where standing there.

They were immediately under interrogation and weren't sure what to say. They could not claim to be the owners of the cabin, and Larry was already in the patrol car because he was caught running down the country road shouting. Jim knew their fun was over and scribbled a note on the back of his fake ID card, which read, "We are in jail." That statement was a prediction of the future, and in his condition, nothing was very clear in his mind.

Jim, Larry, and Earl were in the backseat of the police car when they stopped at a small building somewhere along the highway, but before they knew it, the car continued toward Lake Charles. To be so drunk was unusual for the boys, and the next thing they saw was the inside of a holding cell at the police station. They were given coveralls with C.P.J. stenciled on the back and were told to change into the jail garb. Still not sure what was going on, the boys were placed in cells with bunks for the remainder of the night. They were awakened early the next morning and escorted back to the bull pin for breakfast. It consisted of an aluminum ice cube tray with corn flakes and water.

Back at Jack's camp, the remaining Night Hawks had come to the cabin and found the little scribbled note. They discussed the possibilities and came to the conclusion that the cops had come to the cabin and arrested the three boys. They found a phone and called the parents to let them know what they suspected.

The parents of the three detainees arrived in Lake Charles and found the Calcasieu Parish Jail where the boys had been taken after talking with the local Vinton police.

Earl's dad had driven Jim's mom and Larry's mom from Port Arthur to Lake Charles to help get the boys released. It was not a happy trip back home, and the boys apologized over and over to their parents. Larry and Earl got the appropriate punishment from their parents with restrictions on activities for some time. Jim, on the other hand, came home to wash up and was back out in his hot rod and on his way to see his girlfriend before dark on that Sunday afternoon. There would be no more partics at Jack's camp.

CHAPTER 5

Among Jim's friends in the Night Hawks car club were Gary Carson and Don Downs. Each member of the club had their own distinctive personality that added to the interesting years in high school. Girls liked Gary, and he could date about any of them he wanted, such as a pretty girl named Beth. She was cute, blonde, and bubbly. She fell in love with Gary and became devoted to him. Once he had them interested, Gary would start to neglect them and take them for granted. He told Beth that he would come by her house on Friday night, and at ten p.m. he was still making the drag on Proctor Street with his friends. When asked about Beth, he said, "She is waiting at home for me to come over." Beth tolerated his behavior for months, thinking that he loved her, until she could not take it any longer. After crying for so many nights waiting for Gary, she realized that she deserved more than the way she was being treated. As soon as he realized that Beth was not waiting on him anymore,

Gary was concerned with how Beth felt and tried to win her back by calling and going by her house. When she would not have anything more to do with him, he would peel out in front of her house every night in his 1958 Ford. Because of the strain on the engine and transmission of the Ford, mechanical breakdowns resulted in repair costs for him or his dad. Gary's recklessness went back to his younger days. He had ridden a horse that belonged to his grandfather so hard that it almost died. He thought that a horse could run for hours just like in the movies. His sister Becky once remarked that Gary was born a hundred years too late; he should have lived in the cowboy days rather than in modern times. He was a problem child and tried to do his thing most of the time.

When he was only five years old, Gary's mother took him to school. She returned home and found that he had beaten her there. He got into a little trouble with his father when his older brother bought some cigars and they were caught smoking them behind the garage. Gary was able to shift most of the blame to his older brother and once again did not get the punishment that his brother received. Some years later, Gary had access to a 1954 Ford truck with the family company name painted on each door. It was fun to drive because it would peel out and get rubber in second gear. So Gary drove like a wild man until one night while racing cars on Eleventh Street, Don Downs wanted to drive it in one of the races. When Don tried a speed shift into second gear, he dropped a transmission (in the language of the day) by stripping second gear. It was still drivable enough to get home, and Gary lied to his father by saying, "Something happened to the transmission on the truck, and

I don't know how it could have happened." Again, his lies got him out of trouble, and he did not have to pay for the mistake.

His dad was able to buy him out of trouble, such as the time Gary drove the company truck without permission or a driver's license, which resulted in a wreck and a later incident when he shot-out some store window on Sixteenth Street. Gary made promises to others that he did not intend to keep, and Becky was an easy target for his manipulation. About that time, the family had only one car, a 1955 two-door hard top Bellaire V-8 with a two-tone paint job. Gary and Becky were supposed to share the car or make sure the other had a ride when needed. He promised to pick her up after school, and he did not show up, which forced Becky to walk all the way home. He even removed the hubcaps to make a little money and told his dad they had been stolen. Late one Friday night after talking Becky into letting him take the car for his date, he hit a tree on Seventh Street and totaled the beautiful Chevrolet. He was hurt pretty bad and was exonerated concerning his reckless high-speed driving. His father decided to purchase a black two-door 1950 Chevrolet for Becky, so she would have transportation to high school and college, but Gary took over the car and modified it until Becky was again without transportation. When Gary would get into trouble, his father got him out by using his influence as a former judge and his contacts around the city. His life developed around cheating, lying, and manipulation.

After he got over Beth the best he could, he dated Patsy Tyler, who was popular with mutual friends and was in school organizations in a Catholic school. He treated her well for a while until she was committed to him, and then he began his usual routine. Patsy was a pretty girl who was part of the drill team. In those days the performing group of girls was called a Drum and Bugle Corps. She sat home on weekends while Gary ran around on her. Being devoted to Gary, she ignored the advice of her friends and advances of other boys who wanted to take her out. Don Downs, short, pimply faced, and nerdy, was one of the boys who wanted to date Patsy but had no chance whatsoever. He kept calling her on the phone and going by her house, even though she turned him down time after time. Her girlfriends may have influenced her decision, or it might have been Don's persistence, but she finally agreed to go on a date with him. He had money to spend on girls because of his well-to-do family, and he was financially able to do everything possible to impress her.

Most of the couples liked to park somewhere to explore the opposite sex and develop their young loves. It started with talking, then kissing, then petting, and possibly sex, but more than likely not. If a couple went together long enough and there was a chance of marriage later, the parking could lead to sex, but there were no birth control pills, diaphragms, or IUDs available, and condoms (rubbers to the boys) were not widely used by teenagers.

By the time Don persuaded Patsy to go on a date, they were seniors in high school but did not attend the same school. It started like most dating in the late 1950s with a movie and making the drag with friends. Don asked Jim and Becky to go along to make it easier to talk and get acquainted better. It progressed to more alone time after a few dates, and they did some local parking. On Pleasure Pier Island there was a site overlooking the Sabine Lake, and the kids liked to park there and "watch the submarine races," they called it. During the months of dating, they began to drive to the beach at night and find a secluded place to spend long hours together. Don was very experienced with sex from his visits to the houses of prostitution in Port Arthur, so after a while, he was able to get past Patsy's defenses, and she became pregnant before graduation day. Don had full intentions of marrying her and may have felt that she would surely say yes if she was expecting a baby. There was no chance of an abortion because it was illegal, and she was Catholic, so she would never consider it.

Don and Patsy were married in a private ceremony just after graduation, and the baby arrived three months later. Not even Jim and Becky were invited so that it could be said that they had been secretly married for the last six months. Don's parents furnished an apartment behind the Downs' residence so the young couple could start their adult lives.

CHAPTER 6

Jim and Becky got together in a different way than Don and Patsy. Gary Carson and Jim Gray were members of the Night Hawks together but were barely friends. Gary used the family 1955 Chevrolet Bellaire two-door hardtop for dating. Becky also used the same car to go out with her girlfriends and to drive the two of them to school. As was his nature, Gary contrived a way to get the car by introducing Becky to Jim. An opportunity arose when Becky needed a ride home from school and Gary asked Jim to take his sister home in his begging way. A ride home was all it was for Becky, and doing a favor for someone was all it was for Jim, but Gary had other ideas. Gary pushed for more contact and somehow arranged a date for Jim and Becky on a Friday night so he could have the car. The date went all right, and Gary used his lying ways to try to keep them dating so he could have the car all of the time.

Jim had an accident while driving the Merc to

a Night Hawk meeting that did major damage, and, having only liability insurance, it was going to cost too much to get it fixed. The day after the wreck, Gary and Becky came by to offer Jim a ride to school, and that was another chance for Becky to be around Jim. Later, when Gary took the car and Becky had no ride, Jim Gray and Julie Taylor, his next-door neighbor, would give her a ride to school on occasion. Becky would sit next to Julie in the front seat of the car but wanted to sit next to Jim. She finally got her chance when Julie did not ride with Jim one morning.

There was a rare occurrence in Port Arthur when, in the middle of the night, it snowed enough to cover the ground. For some reason, Jim woke about five a.m. the morning of the snow and wanted to call Becky to tell her. When she came on the line, Jim excitedly told her about the phenomena taking place outside while Perry Como sang "Catch a Falling Star" on the radio that Becky kept by her bed. The high school kids still went to school, but the sight of the white stuff outside enticed them to leave school between classes and embark on an adventure. Some of the usual group, which included Jim, Gary, Prue, Becky, Burl, and Don, headed to the Pleasure Pier Island to play in the snow. They threw snowballs and tried to build a snowman until Becky got too cold and went to the car to warm up. While she sat in the car and watched Jim play with his friends, she decided that she loved him and wanted to spend the rest of her life with him. Their first date was a double date to the Don Drive-in Theater. The show was faded and hard to see, so Jim tried to make out with Becky, but she put up a fight about petting and anything beyond kissing. They dated some during the winter of 1957 into the 1958 school year while Jim dated a few other young ladies.

The Mercury V-8 engine was the heart of his beautiful ride, so he decided to transfer the engine to a 1950 Plymouth that his mom drove to work. The installation had never been done before, and mating the Merc engine to a Plymouth transmission and rear end was said to be impossible. Impossible for Jim meant it would take a little longer to do. Gary showed up one day while Jim was working on the project and made fun of Jim by telling him he would never get it done. Jim was in no mood for Gary's mouth, so he popped him a good one, much to his surprise. He left without a word but soon found out that Jim got it done, and the new combination of Mercury engine and Plymouth body could outrun his car with no trouble. His mouth continued to be a problem when he announced to a group of hot rodders gathered on Proctor that Jim was screwing his sister. Jim grabbed Gary by the front of his shirt and said just as loud as Gary had done, "Why would you say that about your own sister?" Because of and in spite of Gary's selfish manipulations to get the full use of the family car, Jim and Becky dated, and a long-term love developed.

Becky graduated two years before Jim and went to work at her dad's office. She continued to live at home except for a brief attempt to share an apartment with some girlfriends from high school who had also gone to work. Meanwhile, Jim attended his last two years of high school and dated some of the girls in his class and a couple of other girls from lower grades. A few days after graduation, he left for LeTourneau Technical College in Longview but headed back to Port Arthur almost every weekend for dates with

Sharon, Becky, and Karen. Old dorm 4A was part of the run-down campus that was once an army hospital. Mr. LeTourneau had acquired the property from the government to offer industrial skill training to the veterans returning from the Korean conflict. At first, the school offered classes so that a veteran could learn electrical wiring, carpentry, and machine shop trades that would help them get good jobs after serving their time in the military. Jim wanted the technical courses in engineering without going to Lamar University, which his friends called the thirteenth grade. It had been a difficult decision as to whether Jim would go to college because of the cost and the continuation of school, which he did not like very well anyway. LeTourneau seemed to offer just what Jim wanted, and he was assigned a roommate in dorm 4A on the main street of campus. He got permission to go home for the weekend because he lived in the state, while many of the students were from faraway places and could not get such a weekend pass. Once he was told that he could go home on the weekend, he took it for granted that he could go home any weekend and anywhere he wanted without getting another pass.

Jim had wanted a motorcycle for many years. His mom refused to allow any motorbikes, motorcycles, or scooters in the household. She forbid Jim from riding with Lloyd on his motor scooter, but Jim could not resist jumping on the back of the scooter any time Lloyd came by his house. Lloyd eventually had a wreck by hitting a parked car and going on a little flight. Lloyd's broken arm convinced him that it was time to move on to cars.

The boys in the next dorm had an old Harley motorcycle, and Jim became fascinated with it, even though he had never ridden a big bike. When they told him it could be purchased for $150, Jim went into action to sell anything he could to purchase the machine and came up with the asking price. Jim took possession of the old Harley knucklehead while it was still running, and he asked his roommate if he would like to go for a ride. Jim was wearing blue jeans, a white T-shirt, very dark glasses, and a red jacket, while his roommate had only a T-shirt with his jeans. They rode to the nearest gas station to make sure the bike had a full tank and shut off the engine to pump the fuel. It all went well until it was time to start the bike again, and that is when the boys realized that neither of them knew how to start it. It took a while to come to the conclusion that the transmission had to be in neutral and the clutch had to be engaged for the engine to start. Having mastered that little hurdle, they decided to take a run to Dallas on the newly acquired ride. It was only 150 miles, it was almost dark, and by the time they had gotten about halfway there, it had begun to rain heavily. The bike was a 1939 Harley motorcycle with tank shift and no front fender. The seat was big enough for one person, and there was a little luggage rack big enough for a person to sit on over the half-rear fender. It had straight exhaust and no windshield, but what fun to blast down the highway on the two-wheeled hot rod! The rain and cold began to wear on the boys, and they wondered what could be done to overcome the situation. They finally stopped and took a motel room to get warm and dry. The next day was much better, and they rode into Dallas to see a friend for a possible place to sleep over. The friend was happy to see them but had to go to work at a medical center and would be gone the rest of the night. The boys relaxed the rest of the day and had a good night's sleep after the hard trip through the darkness and rain. When morning came, it was time to leave Dallas for Longview and try to get back for classes. The streets of Dallas were loaded with cars during what was called the rush hour; Jim had never seen one before. The two could not sit in heavy traffic in the morning sun, so Jim took to the sidewalk on his loud bike and dodged the pedestrians until he could make it to open roads again. All was going well until the engine started acting strangely about the time they got past the city limits of Dallas. A few stops and re-starts brought them to a shopping center, and there was an automobile service store on the mall parking lot. Jim left the bike next to the building, and the boys walked over to the highway to hitchhike back to school.

They made it back later that night and were able to attend classes the next morning. Jim planned a return trip toward Dallas on the following day to retrieve the bike. He hitchhiked alone to the bike's location. He cleaned the spark plugs and filled it with gas for the anxious trip back to dorm 4A.

Becky and Jim had been dating off and on for years now, and she came to Longview along with Paula Todd and Patsy Tyler for a weekend. Boys from the dorm were easily recruited for a trip to Bossier City and "The Strip," a line of nightclubs along old Highway 80 through part of the area. Clubs with names such as the Blues and the Starlight would let kids in at almost any age, so college students had no problem at all. The trip over in Becky's car was fun while the kids visited and became acquainted. Jim drove Becky's 1960 Chevrolet Impala convertible, which was white with a turquoise interior. They completed the run in about two hours and pulled into the Twilight Club just after dark. The club featured a dark bar area with music and dancing as entertainment. The bar was out in the lobby something like a movie theater, and Jim ordered a Zombie for Becky and himself while the others ordered what they wanted to drink. As the bartender poured the 151-proof rum into the tall Zombie glasses, the top came off, and he spilled an extra amount into the glasses. Needless to say, the kids were off to a roaring start. The plan was to move to various clubs to see the different set-ups and entertainment, a change of atmosphere for the group. Sometime later that night, they entered the Twilight Club, which was off the strip in a different part of Bossier City. Jim had been there before, so he knew what to expect. It was a cozy place with booths and good music for dancing. While Jim danced with Becky, she was overcome by the drinks and fainted dead away. Jim held her up and headed to the back door and the safety of the car. He signaled to the group to head out with him, and they soon followed to see what had happened to Becky. She was out cold and could not be revived, so Paula and Patsy wanted to get a room as quickly as possible. A small motel was found on the highway, and one of the girls checked them in. By the time the girls got Becky into the room, they would not allow Jim to get close to her, and the boys had to sleep in the car while the girls defended the room. The night passed slowly, but the group was able to drive back to Longview the next morning. From Longview, the girls had planned to go on to Austin and other stops, so they said good-bye and took Becky and her hangover out the front gates of the technical college.

On another trip to Bossier City some months later, Jim's car was loaded with guys from dorm 4A and dorm 5A. There were three guys in the backseat, and one guy name Roe Adams had brought a bottle of vodka. He passed it around but also boosted, "I can drink this stuff like water," and proceeded to show the group of boys. By the time they reached the outskirts of Shreveport, Roe and the rest wanted to make a roadside pit stop. Roe staggered over to the ditch next to the road and promptly fell in headfirst. He had to be dragged out of the water and mud because he was stoned and had passed out. Roe was placed in the backseat again, and the group made it to the Bossier City strip. After a little more drinking at one of the clubs, another of the group called Chips had developed problems. He related his life story to the others, which included that his dad was a television personality who had a parrot. The parrot was named Mr. Chips, and his friends had picked up the name to tease him. He had an ulcer, as the group found out, and he began to bleed from the mouth. Chip said that milk helped the condition, so Jim headed to his friend's house. Jim had to wake Lloyd and ask for his help in the situation, but Jim had done the same for Lloyd some years before when he had showed up at Jim's house to avoid going home drunk. Lloyd gave Chip some milk, and his condition improved in a few minutes, so they begin talking about heading back to school, if Chip was up to it. The boys arrived late that night at the dorm 4A and woke some people in the process, and one of them was the dorm monitor for dorm 5A. The next day, the boys from 4A were in trouble for leaving the campus without a pass and coming home drunk and loud. Jim was implicated as being the driver of the Bossier City run and was soon in trouble too. The disciplinary committee had each of the boys come into a room as they were questioned. Jim was expelled for leaving campus without obtaining a pass, and others in the group were expelled for drinking. Jim stayed around Longview for a few days trying to find a job so that he would not have to go home and tell his mom that he was no longer in school, but finally he packed his belongings and started back to Port Arthur to deliver the bad news.

CHAPTER 7

It was 1962 and Jim would be turning twenty years old in April when he began to think about asking Becky to marry him. He was going to night school and was working at Burton's shipyard so they could make a home with the steady income. He rode his motorcycle to town and went into a jewelry store on the corner. He selected an engagement ring with a single diamond and a wedding ring with a twist that fit against the other. The diamond was not very big, but he was excited to be taking this step and he felt that going into big debt for a ring right now would not be wise. He turned his black Harley motorcycle toward home but felt that he just had to show the ring set to someone. He thought of a friend who lived on the way home so he detoured a couple of blocks to Lakeshore Drive and found Norman in his garage with his new Pontiac two-door hardtop Bonneville. He showed Norman the ring set, and they discussed the details of Jim getting married at his age. Jim and Norman had become friends after an introduction by Don Downs some years before. He lived with his parents in a large plantation-type home with multiple floors and big columns supporting the front porch. The grand homes along Lakeshore Drive overlooked the inter-coastal canal and the Pleasure Pier Island. It may go without saying that Norman's family had money and belonged to the country club with the Downs family.

Jim asked Becky to go with him to a movie downtown that night. He went to get her, and they drove downtown. After parking, they walked by Gordon Jewelry and stopped to look at the rings in the window. She pointed out the ones that she liked, and when they continued their walk to the movie house, Jim said, "Those are nice rings, but how do you like this one?" as he held up his hand with a diamond ring on his little finger. The answer was yes, and they never made it to the movie because they went home to tell Becky's parents about the engagement.

The plan was to have the wedding in August when Jim had a long weekend from his work at Burton Shipyard. He was working nine-hour days and did not want to take off too much time for a little trip they had planned. August 31, 1962, was only six weeks away, and the ladies did a good job of putting together a wedding and reception in such a short time. Jim's old friend Larry was his best man, and the small wedding party included friends and family of the couple. Their car had been hidden at a friend's house for safekeeping, and no one knew where it was or it would have been decorated with slogans and such, as was the custom of the day. After the reception, the plan was to have Larry drive them to the car that was ready for the honeymoon trip, but there was a secret plot to block the car in while their friends decorated it.

The plan almost worked, except Jim cut across a neighbor's yard and hit the road out of town. With the friends chasing after, the parade soon drew the attention of the local police, and the newlyweds were stopped for speeding. After a lecture, a threat of jail, and a stern warning, they continued on their way, as it became late at night. The kids drove all night toward Hamilton, Ohio, where Jim had gone to school in the ninth grade. He had kept in touch with friends that would furnish a place to stay for a couple of days. The trip was an exciting adventure of being on their own, and they returned to plan the move into their new house in Nederland, Texas.

Their house in Nederland was being built as the two took their meager honeymoon trip. It was a small light-colored brick house with three bedrooms and single-car garage. Jim had saved money through payroll deduction and used that to purchase the small residential lot, and the house plans had been suggested by the builder to fit the lot. It was very exciting for the young couple to furnish their new home. Some of the furniture was early marriage-type stuff donated by Becky's parents, and some was carefully selected to fit the house. Jim's idea of a kitchen table was one with Formica top and chrome legs, but Becky had the good taste to select a hard-rock maple table with captain chairs for the dining area. Her taste also served well to select hard-rock maple bedroom furniture and canapé bed. Jim could see her talent and learned from it.

Cooking was another area where they both needed improvement. Becky's mother had not taken the time to teach her kitchen skills, and Jim had only learned to cook what he liked, which was steak and canned vegetables. When they tried to cook anything but the basic meal, difficulty ensued. Some food was overcooked, even burned, while other dishes just did not taste like Mama cooked them. Jim's mother did not cook some things, like good Cajun gumbo. Becky's mother did but had not taught her how to do it. When Jim and Becky tried their hand at gumbo, it was bland and lacked something they knew should be there. Making the delightful soup takes hours of preparation and cooking to give it that spicy, tasty quality. No matter what they tried, it just did not taste good, so Becky called her dad and he stopped by on his way to a job site. He re-made the rue and added it to the pot while instructing them on the fine points of making gumbo. After the mixture was simmered for several hours, it tasted much more like real gumbo. The skill and experience of cooking grew over the years, and they won first prize in a gumbo contest many years later.

Jim Gray worked at Gulf Port Shipbuilding at the time Becky was expecting their first child. It was a typical workday for Jim, and he felt that going to work was necessary now that Becky had left her job to have their first child. She asked him to stay home that morning because she was getting near delivery time, but Jim knew that every hour he missed work would just put them farther in debt. The new house was great to have, but there were house notes, car notes, furniture notes, and utilities that were too much for the young father-to-be. Even though Jim's mother had repeated her suggestion to live on one salary, they had not heeded her advice. Now with only one income, times were getting tight for the little household. Jim headed for the old car that he drove to work each day as Becky asked one more time if he would stay home today. A couple of hours after Jim started work at the shipyard, he received a call from Becky that the baby was ready to be born. He rushed to the parking lot and sped home to get Becky.

When Jim arrived at the house, Becky was ready to go, and he loaded her and an overnight bag into the black Cadillac that was part of their two-income purchases.

The hospital was named St. Mary's and was the same hospital where Becky and Jim were born. It was one of the happiest days of his Jim's life, as anyone would well know if they have at least one child of their own. It was extremely exciting when the nurse approached Jim and said, "It's a boy."

When Mitch was brought down the hall in a plastic-covered cart shortly after delivery, his head was pointed. Not seeing a newborn child before, Jim Gray did not know what to think, but Dr. Robertson assured him that the condition was temporary, and it was not uncommon for a baby to have a "cappet." The reason little Mitch had the cappet was the delay in delivery caused by Dr. Robertson having two more patients ready for delivery at the same time little Mitch was trying to come into the world. Dr. Robertson was also late getting to the hospital because he was busy working on one of his antique cars. The wife of an old family friend named Charles Rodman was chosen to go first by the tardy doctor while Becky had to wait. Mitch's head had to pay the price, and it may have been the cause of his special personality and some of his disabilities that showed up later.

After about three days, his parents were able to take little Mitch home in their black 1959 Cadillac to a new house in Nederland, Texas, on South Fifteenth Street, where the nursery was ready for the homecoming. The little brick house was cozy with central air and heat, champagne-colored carpet, and new baby furniture arranged in the spare bedroom. The next few months went along as would be expected, with adjustments for the new baby in the house and extra bills that seemed to be getting higher and higher.

Jim was working for about $2.50 per hour as a draftsman when the little fellow arrived. There was little hope for a raise or advancement at Gulfport, so he sent résumés to every possible prospect for employment. A friend in Longview, Texas, who worked for Eastman Kodak, agreed to help Jim get an interview as a draftsman where he worked. Jim, Becky, and Mitch drove to Longview to interview for a job and, after finishing at Eastman, decided to drive another thirty miles to Lone Star, Texas, to put in an application at Lone Star Steel. Even though it was a cold call, the personnel people invited him to meet the engineering manager, tour the plant, and fill out an application for employment. It seemed like forever, but a job offer was received some months later, about the time the family was on their last leg in Nederland. Becky and Mitch stayed in Port Arthur to try to sell the house while Jim took the job and moved into a little motel in Lone Star for around fifteen dollars a week. The place was more like the old tourist courts of earlier days, except it was in worse shape. It was a depressing place, but Jim spent his time studying a correspondence course that had been started while in Nederland.

Selling the house in Nederland seemed to take forever, and out of more than $4,000 invested in 1962 money, only $200 was recovered. The only consolation was that the family had a fresh start, and the pay was better at Lone Star Steel. They liked the lakes and woods and were able to buy a three-bedroom reconditioned house at the very reasonable price of $4,800.

Another addition to the family came in the form of a Rat Terrier puppy named Mickey. What a pair he and little Mitch became. They had adventures in the woods and around Lone Star that were the subject of a couple of short stories written for little Mitch's amusement. The family lived in Lone Star from the winter of 1964 until the house was sold and a new mobile home was purchased in 1966 to allow Jim to go back to school at LeTourneau College in Longview. Everything in the house was sold and even the boat in the yard so he could go back to school while still working at Lone Star Steel. By working three days a week and going to school three days a week, Jim and his family were able to make it pretty well. Becky decided to go back to work to help with the high tuition and allow Jim to cut back on the number of hours worked each week, while little Mitch had to go to daycare for the first time. Little Mitch had a hard time not being with Becky at home all day and with dad's need to study every night to stay in school. He and Mickey took a couple of unscheduled trips that had the fire department and all the area CB radio operators searching Longview.

One such trip resulted from his desire to see what was in the domes at the LeTourneau factory, which was in sight of where the family lived. He had been promised that he could go see them someday, but when Jim got home from work one night, he was nowhere to be found. His parents got on the CB radio and involved everyone who would help. The local police and others looked for him everywhere, even across the busy highway where the family lived. It was early evening when they were told that he had been found at one of the domes by the security guard and that his parents could come and get him. After getting him from the guard, he was asked why he had left home by himself, and he said, "I wanted to see the domes."

Another such time, the family lived across from the LeTourneau College campus. He and Mickey came up missing again, so his parents called the police and fire department to help search for them. A couple of hours later, little Mitch and Mickey showed up in front of the mobile home riding in a fire chief's car.

The alter-day work schedule went well until about 1968, when Lone Star Steel had a nine-month strike that would require Jim to quit work or quit school. Neither of the alternatives was acceptable, so he began planning a transfer to Lamar University in Beaumont, Texas. Fortunately, Mr. Carson suggested they move the mobile home into a corner of their yard in Port Arthur, and Mrs. Carson would let Becky take her job at Saybolt to help with the living expenses. Shortly after the move, Jim obtained a Tankerman's license, and Mr. Carson was able to arrange jobs for nights and weekends, which made the whole plan work. Mitch stayed with Mrs. Carson during the day and started school at Tyrrell Elementary in Griffin Park in September 1970.

CHAPTER 8

The teachers at school seemed to like Mitch because he was a pleasant kid and loved to do projects that involved artwork. It was not too long before his parents were called in to discuss his difficulties with reading and writing; the school counselors called it learning difficulties. They wanted to give him tests to determine why he had trouble with reading and writing while verbally he could give the answers to questions about what was being studied. His reading was slow and sometimes his writing was backward or some of the words were abbreviated instead of being complete.

Jim graduated from Lamar University in June of 1971 and took the first engineering job in Orange, Texas, at Levingston Shipyard. The family moved the mobile home to West Orange, and Mitch went to the elementary school near the trailer park. It seemed that the teachers at this school let Mitch get by on personality because his parents did not hear much about his learning problems until Jim took a job in Brownsville,

Texas, and the family moved to Harlingen, Texas, in September of 1972.

The teachers in Harlingen requested that his parents come in to his school to discuss more tests and the possibility of special education. The tests did not indicate that Mitch had extreme learning disabilities, so no special measures were recommended by the school. He did not get along well with the Mexican kids at school because he would not stand up to them. He just did not want to fight, and it seemed that little boys liked to pick on those who would not fight back. Mitch developed a dislike for school in Harlingen, but the family was only there for one year and moved to Clear Lake City near Houston in September 1973, so Jim could take a job in medical research in Galveston.

The move was a good one for everyone, including Mitch. The Carsons lived only a block away, which delighted Mitch, who could ride his bicycle over to see PaPa and MaMa Carson, his grandparents. The schools and teachers in Clear Lake were also good for Mitch. He had neighborhood friends, and the family attended a good church, where he made more good friends. After a year, the Carsons moved to downtown Houston to be near PaPa's work because they had been renting the house in Clear Lake. The Gray family purchased a house on Seaside, which was two doors down from the house they had rented for the first year after the move from Harlingen. Being on a cul-de-sac, they visited with neighbors and enjoyed the close community for around five years. About that time, Jim and Becky decided to add to their family, but during her pregnancy Becky had a miscarriage and her ovaries had to be removed in an emergency procedure to save her life. There would be no additional children for the little Gray family, and Mitch would be the only child for the rest of his life.

In 1977, Jim found himself unemployed and took a job doing medical research on the northwest side of Houston, while Clear Lake was on the south side of Houston. The drive became too much after a while, and Becky was ready for a new house, so it was decided to move to Tiger Lane in the Rolling Fork addition in northwest Houston. The move started a bad time for Mitch because he had to leave his friends in Clear Lake, and he was getting to the teenage years. Maybe new friends were getting hard to find, or maybe the new neighborhood kids were part of the problem.

Mitch was about thirteen years old and was not adjusting well to the northwest side of town. The trouble seemed to start with a family named Terry who lived about a block from the new house. Dad found a couple of the boys taking something from Mitch's bike, and he wasn't trying to stop them. He developed a hatred for the school bus, and it could have been the Terry boy or some other bullies on the bus that made him find every excuse for not riding it. Mitch would not tell his dad why he would rather skip school than ride the bus, but he would procrastinate so that his mother or dad would have to take him to school. His parents tried everything they could think of to get him up, dressed, and off to school, but when Becky started back to work, he would hide out until the house was empty and then come back home. When they found out about every new ploy, his parents would take steps to stop him from being late or skipping school altogether.

Mitch began to have increasing trouble in school, which led to punishment from the teachers and principal. His parents could not seem to correct the problem but agreed with the teachers when they were called in for discussions about his behavior. There were several spankings at school administered by Mr. Oliphant, the principal, and numerous calls and notes from school to upset his mom on a regular basis. His dad would try to help him with schoolwork and understand the problem, but Mitch would not let them show him how to do the work, nor would he discuss his problems in detail.

Mitch was the kind of boy who always got caught when he tried to do something wrong. His dad received a call at work one day, and it turned out that Mitch was at home when he should have been at school and had taken Grandmother Gray's car to the store. While backing out, he hit a man's car, and he was at the house at that time. Dad left work and drove home to find that Mitch was trying to give the man a stereo in payment for the damage. His dad paid the man what he thought would cover the damage, and the whole thing was resolved.

The Grays were involved at a church in Jersey Village, which had good influence on Mitch. His mom and dad were the high school department leaders, and Mitch became involved with good young people in the Sunday school group. The young people formed a fun band called Marion Tomacheske and the Polanders to entertain at the Sunday school parties. Mitch played the drums in the band, and it seemed to fit him very well. As part of the act, Mitch imitated a drummer character named Animal from *The Muppet Movie,* and it drew lots of attention, which is what he wanted. His keen sense of humor, his ability to express himself with art, and his laid-back style made people want to be around him. Mitch was about six foot four inches tall by that time and often wore his hair long. He even grew a beard in high school, and everyone knew him for his kindness and wit. He was not looking for a fight, so naturally most people liked him. Mitch was an interesting character, so most everyone knew him at church and in high school.

In 1976, Jim purchased a new Corvette in Clear Lake City, and the kids really loved it. By 1978, he had decided to trade it for a new Buick for Becky because Jim had a company car, and the 'Vette just sat in the garage. Mitch was about fourteen or fifteen years old and had decided that the 'Vette was going to be his car, and he would drive it to school when he got his driver's license. After the trade was made, there was a bad reaction about getting rid of the 'Vette, and he walked out of the house on Tiger Lane. He was gone all night and said that he had walked the twenty or thirty miles to the Buick dealer to get the 'Vette back, not knowing that the car had immediately been taken away by a wholesaler. Mitch and his dad had many discussions about how he could not give him the 'Vette because the insurance would have been impossible. Jim told Mitch that they would build a car for him that would be cooler than a Vette, and his reaction was, "What could be cooler than a Vette?" Dad had in mind to assemble a kit car or something like that, so they started looking for the project vehicle. Mitch did not have much mechanical ability, and Jim thought that would help him learn about cars and bring them closer together at the same time. They visited some local hot rod shops and talked about old cars while they decided what they were going to do. Mom's brother, Uncle Gary, had the major parts for a fiberglass T-Bucket in his garage in Woodville, Texas, as was discovered on a trip to MaMa and PaPa's place in the woods. Gary said that he would take $1,000 for the frame, body, engine, and transmission, which started Mitch and his dad dreaming about hot rodding in a 1929 T-Bucket. It turned out to be far from enough usable pieces to build a car, so they sought help from one of the local hot rod shops. The owner said he would help them assemble a car, and meanwhile they could drive a couple of already-assembled T-Buckets that he wanted to sell. One of the cars was black, had red interior, and lots of chrome, and they loved it. The other was drivable, but unfinished, still in primer and had no upholstery, and they considered it.

The parts that were bought from Uncle Gary were delivered from Woodville to Houston with great hopes for a complete car before too long, but the shop owner said that the frame was the wrong quality, the front axle would never do, and the drive train would not fit into a T-bucket. Their excitement was dampened, but they still wanted a project car and all they had was the wrong parts. The shop owner agreed to trade the unfinished T-bucket they had driven for $2,500, plus the parts that had been brought from Woodville. The money used to buy the car had a symbolic meaning to them. When Grandmother Gray sold her house in Port Arthur, she divided the money between the three living children, and it was that $2,500 that was used to buy the T-Bucket.

They had a T-Bucket of their own, and Jim had gained Mitch's attention. Even if it was not a beauty yet, they had great plans for the little hot rod. They drove it around the neighborhood, and Mitch understood that it was his car.

While driving it around one day, they passed two boys in Jersey Village, and one of them shouted, "All right!" Mitch turned to Jim and said, "Dad, this is cooler than a 'Vette."

Over the next few years, the '29 Ford T-Bucket with the Pontiac 400-cubic-inch, tri-powered engine developed into a beautiful vehicle with a light blue paint job and blue upholstered interior. It had the things Mitch liked, such as a stereo radio, pinstripes, and an *aooga* horn. It would turn heads when Mitch drove by, and just in case someone did not give the car his or her full attention, the surprising horn would do it, *aooga.*

The hot rod car, Mitch's personality, and his unusual appearance gained him recognition around northwest Houston. He once remarked when his dad had to ground him and would not let him drive for some period that the T-Bucket was "him," like it was his soul. His dad always thought if Mitch's ghost was going to haunt something, it would be that car.

After Grandmother Gray sold her house in Port Arthur, she came to live with the family in an apartment behind the house on Tiger Lane. Mitch helped to keep her company, but after a while, she developed a problem with memory and what they thought was "old-timer's disease." She would send Mitch to the store for various supplies, and they worked out a deal to get her brandy at the local liquor store. Grandmother Gray was giving checks to Mitch to cash for shopping, and he was able to keep some of the cash.

In 1983, Grandmother went to live with Aunt Gail near Dallas. One day Jim received a call from his sister concerning Grandmother's bank account. She said that it looked like Mitch had taken a lot of money out of her account over a period of time. Aunt Gail sent copies of the checks for review, and Jim wrote back on October 24, 1983, that he had discussed the checks with Mitch and he had agreed to pay back all that he owed the account. Mitch had just started working, and part of his salary was used each payday to reimburse the account. Between Mitch not realizing that he should not be taking Grandmother's money and Grandmother Gray's willingness to give him the money, it had gotten out of hand. In August of 1984, the family received a letter from Grandmother Gray asking for all of her belongings. They packed up everything she had and started checking into the old Dodge Dart's whereabouts. Mitch said it was at Billy's house and that they were rebuilding the engine. Dad went to Billy's and found that the head had been removed from the engine and the car was sitting alongside their house. The car was towed to a shop near the Grays' house, and the repairs came to $639.73. When it was ready, they shipped the car and all of her belongings to Dallas. Communications with Aunt Gail ceased for nearly five years because she thought that the family had abused Grandmother, and the family thought that she wanted all of mother's belongings. Neither was true.

CHAPTER 9

More trouble came by way of Jersey Village High School in the form of a prank Mitch tried to play. It was dumb and ill advised but probably came from his dad's old stories or from the movie "American Graffiti." Boys at Jim's school put firecrackers in school toilets, the same as the boys in the movie "American Graffiti." For excitement or out of frustration from not doing well in school, Mitch poured cleaning fluid into a toilet at school and lit it. As it was all his life, he was caught, and the school did not consider it a joke. It was the final straw for Mitch at Jersey Village High School, and it resulted in him being expelled permanently.

During earlier problem times at school, his parents had taken Mitch to counselors who worked for the school district. After that did not work out, they took him to a psychologist that cost fifty dollars per hour and then finally to a psychiatrist that cost $150 per hour to try to help Mitch with the things that troubled him. Not much was gained by the effort, and the cost was a burden, but two small things were revealed that may have helped his parents deal with Mitch's problems.

During skipping school and other such problems, Mitch decided he was going to leave home. His dad did not know how to react, so he called the psychologist and asked him. He said to let him go and offer to take him to the bus, so Jim did exactly what the doctor said. He went upstairs to Mitch's room while he was packing some clothes and told him that he would take him to the bus station or out on the highway so he could hitchhike to his destination. Mitch backed off quickly when he tried to think about how and where he would live if he left home and realized that his bluff had been called.

Another assessment made by the expensive psychiatrist made sense to Mitch's parents and helped to explain what they had seen for years. The doctor said that after the tests, he felt Mitch was a perfectionist and would rather fail than not do something exactly right. The reason it seemed to be true was that he had refused so many times to try to do homework or go into art more seriously because he did not think he could do it.

After the incident at school, Mitch was sent to Clara Scott, a school set up to deal with kids who had problems in regular school. They had a point system to help control the students by giving them certain privileges when they did well and taking the privileges away when the student did not control themselves.

Mitch met a boy named Billy Edwards at Clara Scott who knew a lady whose name was Gray before she was married. The lady turned out to be a cousin, Patricia Gray, and was the daughter of Granddad's brother, Aubrey Gray. Mitch went to meet the family with Billy and became friends with Patricia's sons and family. He attended church with the family on occasion, and dad was able to talk to them after many years. Granddad Gray died in 1955, and Aubrey had gone a long time ago, so the families did not keep in touch except through an occasional letter between Grandmother Gray and Aubrey's wife.

Clara Scott helped Mitch get through the remaining time in high school with only a few incidents to keep it interesting. His dad had purchased an old Jeep for hunting trips, and Mitch decided to take it to school one day. He was showing off for the class when the Jeep turned over. He and his friend pushed it back upright, and it was still drivable. Another time, Mitch was given permission by his mother to drive the old Jeep to get a hamburger, but he just had to drive through Jersey Village. He drew the attention of a Jersey Village cop because of an expired inspection sticker, so the policeman turned on the red lights. Instead of stopping, Mitch decided to get out of Jersey Village, and he ran stop signs and exceeded the speed limit while heading for home. Maybe Mitch thought he could outrun the police car, or perhaps he thought the Jersey Village cops had no jurisdiction outside of that little community, but they were in hot pursuit. He thought he could lose them by cutting through the neighborhoods and across a narrow footbridge in the old Jeep. The police were not sure that he had stolen the Jeep and decided not to force him to stop but traced the Jeep to the Gray residence. It took a local lawyer and a great deal of explaining in the Jersey Village traffic court to get him off with a few fines.

Mitch was able to get into trouble without any help, but Billy was an accident looking for a place to happen. He was a likeable but brash young man with a rough family life and his own problems at school. He was the type of person Mitch did not need in his life. His parents heard that Billy had wrecked every car and motorcycle he had ever had and nearly killed himself on more than one occasion. In addition to his problems at home, at school, at work, and with the law, Billy had friends he introduced to Mitch. One of these friends, named Bumgarden, moved into the garage apartment behind the Grays' house for a while, and another time Billy left home to live with the Grays until his father calmed down. Billy had two or more sisters, and one of those sisters fell in love with Mitch and would call him all the time. One night Mitch's parents received a call from Mrs. Edwards, and she asked Mitch's parents to stop the romance between Mitch and Anna because her daughter was too young for him. Mitch's parents had a talk with him; Mitch was around eighteen years old, and the girl was fourteen.

The friendship with Billy and a couple of their friends continued over the next few years after high school graduation. The bad influence was still there too. One time the boys disappeared for a couple of days. His parents called around looking for Mitch and found that they had taken Grandmother Gray's 1963 Dodge Dart to Oklahoma. They had car trouble on the road, and their return was delayed while they put another distributor on the old car.

The summer of 1980, the family took a vacation to Colorado and spent a week riding horses in the mountains. It was a great time for everyone, and they were able to take side trips to Durango, Mesa Verdi, and ride on the Silverton train. After a week away from work, school, and the big city, they were on their way home to Houston. Mitch told his dad that the red Firebird was at Tom's house getting a coat of paint. It somehow dawned on Jim that it did not sound like a true story. Jim finally asked him, "Where is your car, and don't lie."

Mitch told his dad, "Billy has the car, but he will take good care of it."

"Don't you know that he will wreck it or damage it?" Jim's said.

When they arrived home, it did not take long for Mitch to find out that Billy had taken the car to Westheimer Road to race, and it had been hit from the rear by another car. The beloved red 1967 Firebird with the 400-cubic-inch tri-powered engine and four on the floor was beyond repair.

Around 1981, Mitch and Billy were stopped by a police officer, and because of the way Billy acted, the car was searched and a marijuana cigarette was found. From that incident, Mitch was on probation for five years and had to see a probation officer with a payment of twenty-five dollars every month. Mitch was not working at the time, and his Firebird was in a shop that Billy had recommended. The boys had a plan to have the engine and drive train removed from Mitch's beloved car and installed in another body by the repair shop.

Mitch decided that he wanted to move to the Lake Somerville area and live in a room to be furnished by someone Billy knew. He packed everything he could take in the T-Bucket and a friend's car and headed to a small town near the lake. He told his parents that he found work at an auto parts store and could drive out to the lake as the sun went down. He thought it was the most beautiful sight he had ever seen. A few months later, he was back at home and living in the garage apartment behind the house on Tiger Lane. On the way back from his adventure, Billy was driving the T-Bucket and was stopped by the police. The T-Bucket was impounded, and the boys did not know how to get the car back and did not have the money for the towing and storage. Jim considered leaving the car there as the days went by but finally realized it was too much of an investment to give away. Mitch had to have his T-Bucket. So in September 1983, Jim drove to the impound yard and paid the amount needed to get the car released, but it went into the garage and Mitch was not allowed to drive it for a while.

The 1967 Firebird Mitch had worked so hard to buy was still at the repair shop, so he had no way to get around except bum a ride from his parents or go with friends like Billy. Jim thought that something must be done, so he forced Mitch to show him where the shop was so he could talk to the shop owner. There was a big plan to buy another Firebird and transfer the drive train to it, but so far nothing had been done, and it seemed that nothing would be done. The shop owner had another red Firebird with automatic transmission and standard engine that he wanted to sell. He agreed to take $2,000 and the remains of Mitch's car in trade. It was not what he wanted, but it was a functional automobile that looked like his red Firebird hot rod.

Somewhere about that time, Jim sat down with Mitch and reviewed his options, something he had done a number of times over the years during and after high school. At one point, he had the option of continuing his education or going to work. He chose to do neither. The present option was to get a haircut or move out. He chose the haircut. As they walked out of the mall where Mitch had received a very stylish haircut, Jim asked, "Have you been looking for a job?"

"Yes," Mitch answered. "I applied at this place right here, Ruby Tuesday." They went into the restaurant, and Mitch approached the manager to inquire about the application. When the manager saw him with a haircut, he was hired on the spot and was to start work on Monday.

For Mitch's twenty-first birthday, his parents wanted to do something nice for him that would enable him to make a fresh start. The Firebird was not exactly what Mitch wanted, and his parents discussed trading it for a newer car, such as a new Pontiac T-1000, which was a small economy car. To try to interest him in a new car and to support his launch into the workforce, his parents rented a small car for a whole month and presented it to him for his birthday. He enjoyed driving the new car and used it to get to work and to earn extra money by delivering pizzas. At the end of the month, something happened to the car, and it was reported stolen and was found burned. The insurance company went crazy, and for a while it seemed as if Mitch's parents were responsible for the car's replacement. Somehow it all went away. His parents suspected that Billy had something to do with the mysterious event.

The scrapes with the law did not stop, and in the summer of 1985, Jim paid $125 when Mitch ran a red light, $250 because they found what was described as drug paraphernalia, and $300 to the Justice of the Peace that was connected to the same incident. Jim questioned Mitch about the incident and asked, "Do you use illegal drugs?" Mitch answered with a little laugh, "Dad, I don't do drugs. The whole thing was a big mistake."

CHAPTER 10

Earl Long was abandoned by his mother and was taken in by a preacher's family in Humble, Texas, near Houston. He was a young boy but already had a bad attitude. Even though the preacher tried to work with him, he was always in trouble. His parents were Mexican migrant workers, so they were constantly moving from job to job in various parts of the country. The steady home life enabled him to go to school on a regular basis, and he succeeded in hiding his cruel personality from both foster parents and teachers. He tormented other kids around the neighborhood and at school, especially the younger, smaller ones. He somehow managed to complete public school and junior college before taking a job at Gulf Oil in Baytown. He married a girl named Amy and had two children, but family abuse was rampant in his household. He slapped and punched his wife when he lost his temper, and he did not care if she knew about his affairs with other women. He bullied his son, Earl Jr., until he was afraid of his father and even other boys at school. He became a first-class coward as well as fat and sloppy. Earl's daughter, Lori, had to grow up with improper attention from her father until she was old enough to leave home at age sixteen. She once was on a church bus, and her father decided that she could not go to church camp and demanded she get off the bus. When the driver hesitated to let the girl leave his care, Earl pulled a gun and went aboard the bus to force his daughter to leave with him. As results of his carousing and cheating on his wife, Amy, for nearly twenty years, he brought one of the other women to his house in northwest Houston to stay. In defiance of his wife's protests, he had the new woman named Bonnie sleep with him in the master bedroom and told Amy to hit the road. She had been submissive for so long and willing to tolerate his abuse until then because she wanted to stay with her family. Earl and Bonnie tried to force her out of the house verbally, but she stayed in the spare bedroom and resisted their attempts to get her out. After a few months, Earl and Bonnie decided to tie her in a chair and make her watch them have sex. As a result of that experience, she agreed to pack her things and leave if they would let her go, and they accomplished their goal of getting rid of Amy.

Earl Jr.'s cowardess at school made him afraid of a brash young man named Billy Edwards, so he reported back to his dad that Lori was living with the Edwards family. Earl called Billy one time to express his opinion about his daughter living there and the conversation ended with bad language and threats from both Earl and Billy. They had never met, but there would be trouble if they ever did. After a couple of years, Lori, married Billy Edwards to satisfy the need for love and protection. Earl, meanwhile, had been forced to retire early from Gulf Oil, and he was none too happy about it. The retirement package enabled him to persue other interests, including a federal firearms license so he could sell guns on the side. His word-of-mouth business did well, and he stocked automatic weapons, pistols, and ammunition. He owned an oozy, a 9mm Browning semi-automatic, and a twenty-five-caliber pistol for personal use.

CHAPTER 11

In the summer of 1985, Tracor, a group out of Austin, Texas, purchased Medical Research Services, the company Jim worked for. This company had also purchased Medinautics, a research group Jim knew in Columbia, Maryland. A job was offered in Columbia, and they decided to take it and move to Maryland, but Mitch did not want to leave Texas and his friends. They discussed his options, and he decided that he wanted an apartment to go with his job and his car, being twenty-one years old. Jim and Becky helped him get into the apartment and supplied the furnishings, advice, and financial help to make him comfortable, while they made the move to Maryland in August 1985.

March 1, 1986, started out like a routine Saturday morning in the Grays' townhouse in Columbia, Maryland. The phone rang about nine a.m., and a voice on the other end said, "Mr. Gray, I'm Gracie, Billy Edwards's sister. I'm at Ben Taub Hospital with Billy, and I've called to tell you that Mitch is dead. Mitch and Billy were both shot last night by Mr. Long. He's Lori's father." Gracie may have explained why this had happened to Mitch, but Jim was not able to comprehend anything she was saying after she said, "Mitch is dead."

Jim called to Becky to come from another room in the house and told her what was being reported. They were both in a state of shock and disbelief. Jim completed the conversation and hung up while the two of them stood by the phone repeating the few known facts about Mitch being dead. The first thought was to get into the car and drive directly to Houston.

While packing and preparing to leave, they called a friend named Debbie in their church and asked her to look after their dog and cat while they were away. She let others in the church know what had happened, and the church family at Covenant Church responded quickly to help the Grays. The deacons came up with $1,000 to help with expenses, and they felt they were making the trip with the love of each church member. Later the preacher flew to Houston and rented a car to attend Mitch's funeral in Woodville.

Jim called his sister in Woodbridge, Virginia, and told her they were heading to Texas. She insisted that Jim and Becky come by her house, and she supplied them with food for the trip and her gas card to help with expenses. Before they left, there was a call from a man in Houston who offered to get Mitch's body released from the morgue and deliver him to the funeral home of their choice. They chose Nunley-Stanley in Port Arthur because of the family burial plots there, and the family knew the funeral home.

When they called Becky's mother and dad, they

asked if they could handle the arrangements and allow him to be buried in Woodville instead of Port Arthur. The Grays were still in shock and welcomed the help.

It is a twenty-four-hour drive from Columbia, Maryland, to Woodville, Texas, if one pushes it as they did. By the time they arrived late on Sunday March 2, 1986, Mitch was already at the funeral home in Woodville, and a cemetery plot had been purchased. Friends from Houston called and visited the Woodville funeral home because they had seen the television report, read the newspaper, and had been informed by other friends that Mitch had been killed.

What a comfort to the Grays to have friends and relatives at a time such as that. Some of the people who attended the funeral were Mitch's friends, Billy's family, and others who knew the Grays from Port Arthur, Houston, and from church. The church in Maryland insisted that the pastor, Dr. Dana Cole, represent them at the funeral in Texas.

A tragedy is a time of emotional hurt. While the Grays were absent from church activities for a week, the members' sacrifices of money to send the preacher as well as the $1,000 became a problem. While they were gone, a lady in the church named Ellen suggested in a meeting that the Grays were doing too much in the church. When they returned to Maryland, the preacher hinted several times that things were going to change and that those affected would have to accept it. In his last visit with the preacher, Jim was told he would never know the sacrifices the church members had made for them. After the preacher called Jim to a committee meeting at his house and told him that he was being replaced as the song leader for the church, Jim repaid the $1,000 and resigned from all the jobs they were doing at the church. Becky lost her job at the church over the incident. The way the changes were done and his state of mind over losing Mitch caused Jim to react very badly, and he never went back to church. The friends they thought cared for them were gone too.

CHAPTER 12

The Grays found out that Billy's little sister had a real love for Mitch, and the feeling seemed to be mutual. They would never know what could have been, as in all cases of a young person dying. Three months short of his twenty-second birthday, Mitch was buried on March 3, 1986, facing west toward the setting sun, in Mt. Pisgah Cemetery in Woodville, Texas. Mitch liked sunsets and told his dad so; he even wrote a postcard telling his parents that he watched a sunset in Galveston. The cemetery plot the Carsons purchased faced east, so Jim asked that Mitch's coffin be turned so that he would face west. Mitch's headstone was at his feet. The night after he was buried, Becky cried harder than Jim had ever seen her cry in all the years he had known her. They had laid their only son, Mitch, to rest, but they were far from personal rest. The Grays still did not know the full story of why Mitch had been killed because Billy was still in the hospital in Houston.

A call came from Dr. Andrews at Medinautic in

Maryland shortly after the funeral and he said, "I'm sorry to be calling at a time like this Jim, but you are needed back at the laboratory." The mourning for Mitch was cut short and they barely had time to clean out his apartment and move his car to the house on Tiger Lane. There was no time to find out what had happened the night he was killed.

About a week later, Billy called from the hospital in Houston. He told Jim, "I am in the hospital and can hardly talk because of the wound in my neck, but I owe you an explanation of how Mitch died."

"Mr. Gray," Billy said, "me and my wife, Lori, brought a girl as a blind date to Mitch's apartment, along with some fried chicken for him." "I knocked on the door and found Mitch at home in his apartment." "I had to just show up because he had no phone in the apartment."

Billy continued in a raspy voice, "I went out to my car to make room by removing some items from the car, such as a toolbox and a work stool my dad gave me for my birthday." "The girls came back to the apartment so I could introduce Margret to Mitch before we went on a little ride in my new blue Ford Mustang." "When we left the apartment, I met Lori's brother as he was moving into an apartment near Mitch's place." "There was an argument between me and my brother-in-law, Earl Long Jr., and it seemed that Earl was scared of me the whole time we talked." "It must have been that as soon as we were out of sight, Earl called his father and told him that I was leaving the apartments in a blue Mustang."

"Earl Sr. must have started toward the apartment complex in a Mazda from his house some five miles away to catch us." "He must have seen us in the car and started chasing us, because a car came up behind me very fast." Billy related the story with some gaps and emotion, saying, "They chased us, and at one time I was looking at three guns pointed at me." "We stopped at the Fairbanks liquor store to call the cops, and Long shot me through the glass." "That's all I remember." "They tell me that Long shot Mitch while he was trying to use the phone to call for help." "Mr. Gray, I am afraid that Mr. Long is still out to kill me so I am in the hospital under an assumed name."

That was all that Jim got from Billy at that time concerning the shooting and murder except, "I am so sorry, Mr. Gray, that Mitch was killed." "He was my best friend, and he died because of me."

Jim wrote Billy a letter trying to let him know that he understood about the friendship he and Mitch had. He told Billy to read a Bible verse in St. John 15:13, where it says, "Greater love hath no man than this, that a man lay down his life for his friends." Jim must have suspected something about that night that was later confirmed during Long's trial.

Jim had told his son that Billy would get him killed, but he expected it to be a car accident, not murdered by someone Mitch did not even know.

CHAPTER 13

Shortly after Mitch's funeral, Becky received a letter from Tess Trahan. She started by saying, my name is Tess. I want to share the precious memories I have that may be a little fuzzy but still tell a story of two friends who had a deep bond. This is a story about a remarkable, unconditional best friend, Mitch Gray. He was and still is, through all the love we have shared, the greatest guy I have ever met.

I was young, sweet sixteen, when I met Mitch. I had heard his name at school many times; he was a legend. We were all rebels in high school, but I think Mitch just wanted to give everyone a good laugh. I was hanging out in the smoking area at Jersey Village High School where everyone was like me. Billy Edwards said, "Hey, there's Mitch Gray in his T-Bucket." That was the first time I saw him. He was tall and had beautiful long hair, and I was immediately attracted to him. And the T-Bucket was baby blue, my favorite color. I wanted a baby blue '65 Mustang. I thought, *Wow, that's Mitch Gray, and I'm going to meet him.*

I don't remember if it was cold outside. I was talking to my friend Billy Edwards that day. He was easy to talk to, and I had not had many good experiences with the kids at school. I got made fun of a lot earlier but not so much in high school, but there was still that feeling of being an outcast. I think that Billy was the same way, too. People used to say that he was slow, but I did not see it. He seemed smart to me and kind of goofy. I think he wanted to be funny to overshadow his dyslexia, and I think he didn't have a lot of self-esteem. A lot of the outcasts hung out in the smoking area.

"Hey, there's Mitch Gray," Billy said. I had to meet him. "Go talk to him," Billy said, nudging me in Mitch's direction.

"Hello," I said. "You're Mitch Gray"—like he didn't know who he was— "I've heard a lot about you and wanted to meet you. You're really into The Doors. Jim Morrison is my favorite."

"Oh yeah? Well ..." he said, playing it cool.

I don't remember another word he said.

I was infatuated. He had the dreamiest eyes and smile, and he was talking to *me.* Because he was what I considered to be the coolest of the cool, I half expected him to ignore me and walk away. The first time I talked to Mitch, he was wearing worn moccasin boots.

Whether Mitch knew how I felt about him or if Billy told him or not, I don't know. All I know is, things were not clear to me after meeting Mitch. My younger sister, Vicki, and Billy's sister, Gracie, were best friends. Vicki and Gracie arranged an outing to a club called Rockabilly, but, in the end, Gracie's dad would not let her go. They told me at the last minute that Mitch was coming, and he would give us a ride home. The girls had set up the meeting, and it seemed that Mitch was in on it. I was so excited.

I was in an air guitar contest, which I lost badly, as I didn't recognize "Our Lips Are Sealed" by the Go-Gos. There was dancing, and between dances our group sat around chatting, feeling so grown up because we were in a dance club. "Waiting for a Girl Like You," by Foreigner, started playing, and Mitch asked me to dance. He was a foot taller than I am, and he held me close, so caringly and so gently. I listened to the words of the song and thought, *I wonder if he has been waiting for a girl like me.* I hoped that he had been.

I could tell him anything, and I did. I close my eyes now and I can still hear his voice.

With all my love,

Tess

CHAPTER 14

The house on Tiger Lane in Houston was placed on the market when the Grays moved to Maryland in 1985, but it did not sell. It was rented out twice, and both times the renters did damage to the house and slipped out owing rent money. Jim made the first trip to Houston to get the house ready to rent for the first time and had Mitch meet him there in January 1986 so they could visit while Jim made minor repairs. They talked and worked on a window seat area to refinish the wood where potted plants had been sitting for years. When suppertime rolled around, they drove to Windfern road to have supper at Lone Star Pizza while they talked about Mitch's job and his finances. Back at the house, Mitch did not feel well and wanted to go back to his apartment because it was getting late. They hugged and said their usual good-byes, and that was the last time that Jim saw him alive. Jim told him, "I love you, son," as Mitch headed out the front door on Tiger Lane.

The next trip to Houston was after Mitch's funeral in Woodville in March 1986 when Becky and Jim moved his things out of the apartment. Their stay was cut short because of an emergency on one of Jim's special projects back at work in Maryland, and that did not help the grieving process to have to rush back to Columbia.

The third trip to Houston, Jim brought his nephew David with him to load Mitch's T-Bucket on a trailer for the trip back to Virginia where David lived. He was good with hot rod cars, so he wanted his cousin's most prized procession for his own, and Jim thought that Mitch would want him to have it. David knew the car well because he had spent a summer with the Grays in Houston while the car was in its earlier stages. The trip back to Virginia included a stop at the Tennessee Valley Authority office in the Blue Ridge Mountains where Jim had some business with a research project that needed his help. It was only a day's delay and then Jim, David, and the hot rod car were on the road again. David turned the T-Bucket into a show car, and it appeared in car shows around the USA. Mitch would have liked that.

Another trip to Houston without Becky took place to get the red 1967 Firebird from a repair shop. The car had been towed to a shop by a friend after the short trip to Houston and Woodville for the funeral. The shop found that only the malfunctioning key switch prevented Mitch from going to work that night in February. One of Mitch's friends called just before he left Houston and wanted to meet Jim while he was in town, so Debbie Kent came to the house on Tiger Lane while the Firebird was being loaded onto a trailer for the trip to Michigan, where Jim had taken a research position in 1988 after the laboratory in Maryland had been closed. Debbie was a petite young lady and must have looked like a midget up against Mitch. The beautiful girl told Jim a little about how she felt about Mitch. She said, "I was in a pleasant state of shock ever since I met Mitch in high school. There was something about Mitch that took my breath away, and I loved him from the first time we met." She also said, "I don't know what to do now that he is gone," and admitted, "My heart aches for him." During the conversation, Jim mentioned, "I will be taking a short trip to Port Arthur and wonder if you would like to come along. We could see where Mitch was born and lived until I finished at the university." Debbie jumped at the chance.

They had lunch at Sartan's, which was a favorite seafood restaurant that served crabs, shrimp, and oysters. Debbie talked about Mitch until she was able to get much of her pent-up feelings out to someone who really cared. The day ended back at the house on Tiger Lane, and Debbie left for home. Jim took the red Firebird back to Michigan and left it with a man named Kasten, who restored old cars. It was not Mitch's first Firebird with the tri-power engine and a four-speed transmission, but it was the one that he had last driven. The car may have cost Mitch his life because he was at home in his apartment when Billy came by instead of being at work at Ruby Tuesday.

Mitch liked to go to record sales that were sometimes held at local hotels. They usually had racks and tables with old records and albums so he could purchase his favorite music. He liked anything by The Doors, Grateful Dead, and ZZ Top. At one of these sales he met a girl named Tammy. She fell instantly in love with Mitch and called his parents' house repeatedly before their move to Maryland. She would ask for Mitch, but Jim did not know that she was the daughter of Jim's boss until later. She met Mitch at every opportunity and kept the secret of her love for him from her father, even after Mitch's death.

Billy's sister Anna was still in school after Mitch graduated and started work, but she continually wrote notes and letters to him. Sometimes Billy would bring the notes to Mitch, and he collected them in his apartment. That is where Mitch's parents found them when they moved his belongings. They were the type of love notes that a young girl writes to her first real love. On October 19, 1984 she wrote:

> Hey Babe,
>
> Hi! Thanks for the letters. They made my whole day. What are you talking about I didn't listen to you again? Oh, never mind I understand! I now understand why you're going to Austin. Maybe when you come back I'll be old enough to date. If you go up to Austin, we can't get in trouble. I'll miss you! I really think you draw better than you write, and I love your lizard! Well, I didn't get this letter at lunch today; I got it this morning at my locker. See, I told you I would be able to figure your letters out. I had no trouble. Now you have to learn to write them longer. What do you mean, "Keep my butt in-line"? Please explain. I love you always! I am glad that you agree about what I said. No one will take you away from me, never! Understand? I don't care if I have to run away to Austin, I will, just to be with you! I haven't spoken to my mom since she found out I was calling you! She yelled at me, so I'm not talking to her. She can't do any-

thing about it! And I have not spoken to Gracie; she's the one that told! Don't worry I got her back. I told Joey that she was gonna go out with Jay R. and he couldn't come back over to our house, so he was pissed. But as usual, they are back together. You should have heard Gracie that day! She told on me, so I won't talk to her. I gave her mean looks and she said, "Anna, I understand you're mad at me and I don't blame you, but I didn't mean to tell on you, but you woke me up at two in the morning." She said, "Please don't tell Joey about me and Jay R," and that is what gave me the idea to tell Joey. You have to see my locker! It's decorated with your name all over it. I'll always love you! Oh, guess what, I want a picture of you. Sorry I got you in trouble. I will start listening to you. I wish I was going to Austin with you, so I'm counting on you to write me. You are all I need. All my love goes to you and no one else. I don't want to let you go, but I have to. I love you! Bye! Forever! Always!

I love you always,

Anna

CHAPTER 15

The trial of Earl Long Sr. came about two years after he shot and killed Mitch and shot Billy in the neck. The family still lived in Maryland, and no official of Houston ever notified the family of Mitch's death. It was difficult to get a trial date or any information about the case by calling down to Houston. A good friend named Shelton Thomas was in the Houston Fire Department and was able to point Mitch's father to the right person to get the first real information about the murder case. There was a case number assigned, and finally an assistant district attorney was assigned to the case. As it works in the Houston courts, a person who is not in jail can postpone his trial date indefinitely because the ones in jail are taking up space. Long had been taken to jail but was out the next day on $10,000 bond. The assistant DA was named Joe Magnum and was willing to discuss the case over the phone with the family and to keep them posted about Long himself. One time Long had the police to his house when he shot his gun and spread catsup around in some fit he was having at the time. Mitch's dad was told that Long thought that he was bad, meaning tough, and would not last long in prison if he was convicted.

The time for the trial finally came, and Jim flew to Houston without Becky. He sat alone in the courtroom while the defendant marched in with his high-priced lawyer named Skip Mandel. Long was portrayed as the retired businessman in his new suits, and Mitch and Billy were portrayed as dangerous hoodlums. When the man who owned the store testified, having seen the whole thing, it was said that he could not be believed because he knew Mitch. When Jim took the stand to tell how gentle Mitch was, the jury was told not to believe him because he was just a prejudiced parent. When Billy took the stand to tell his side of the story, the jury was told that he was a violent young man that might have threatened poor Mr. Long. Now it was brought out that Earl Long Sr., Earl Long Jr., and Bonnie Long all had guns, and Mitch and Billy had no guns. It was testified that the Longs chased Billy and the kids at high speeds until they stopped at the store to call for help, but somehow it was the kids' fault that they were shot. Mitch and Billy were shot with a Browning Hi-Power semi-automatic 9-mm pistol with a thirteen-shot capacity. Mrs. Bonnie Long had a .25-caliber semi-automatic pistol fully loaded, and Earl Long Jr. had a pistol under the seat of his car but denied bringing it out or pointing it at the kids. In the backseat of Long's car was a fully automatic assault rifle with plenty of ammunition, but it was explained that he had a license for it, so it was all right.

The trial lasted a week, and the Long family had perfectly rehearsed testimonies that matched in every detail. Lori, Billy, Margaret, and Gene, the storeowner, testified to what they saw from their various locations. The story was told that Billy was outside being confronted by Long Sr., Lori was in the store trying to use the phone, and Margaret was in the backseat of the Mustang with Mitch near the start of the trouble, after having been blocked in by the three Long vehicles in the parking lot. Mitch tried to get out of the car, and Long told him that if he did, he would kill him. Mitch got out the other side of the car and went into the store to help Lori call for the police on the phone. Mitch knew the storeowner because he worked at an auto parts store two doors down while in high school. The storeowner told how Billy ran into the store to get away from Long Sr., and Long shot Billy through the front glass of the store. Long stepped over to the open door of the store and shot Mitch in the face, which took out part of his brain after the bullet passed through his hand. The assistant DA tried to explain that it was not shooting in self-defense on Long's part, and Mitch was instinctively putting his hand up in front of him. Skip contended that Mitch was some kind of threat to Long, but Jim thought that anyone could see that the kids were chased down by the armed Longs and posed no threat to anyone. Mitch's autopsy showed that he had no drugs, no alcohol, or any illegal substance in his blood, which proved to Jim what Mitch had always said, "Dad, I don't do drugs."

It was late on a cold Friday afternoon, February 5, 1988, when the jury was charged with finding Mr. Long guilty or not guilty. If guilty, the jury would have to determine the punishment, and the trial would continue. Just before the jury left the room, they were told that the roads were getting icy around Houston, a rare occurrence. It did not take long for the jury to come back with a not guilty verdict, and then it was all over and they could go home.

During the jury deliberation, Billy, Lori, Momma Edwards, and Mitch's dad sat in the empty courtroom discussing the testimony, the trial, and the things that had led to the shooting. Billy explained some things that had puzzled Jim, such as why Mr. Long was after them that night and what had happened to invoke the shooting. Briefly the story was told how Lori had run away from her father's house some time before and lived with the Edwards. She and Billy had fallen in love and were married without permission from Long. Billy had never met Mr. Long, but they had spoken on the phone, which resulted in threats from Long Sr. He also explained that Earl Long Jr. was a coward who was afraid of Billy and had told his father everything bad about Billy. The night of the chase, Earl Jr. had called his dad at home and told him that Billy was giving him some sort of trouble, and Earl Sr. ran out of the house in a rage.

Another explanation came up when Billy told how Mitch was his best friend and related something that had taken place five years earlier, when Mitch and Billy came home very late one night. When Mitch's dad woke up that night and went downstairs, Billy's dad was there. He told Mitch's dad that the boys had been arrested and he had gotten them out of jail. Mitch's dad was told that everything was going to be all right and found out later that Mitch had to go to court and was put on probation, but he did not have to do anything. Mitch had to report to the probation officer for five years and had to do civic duty for 180 hours, yet he always had a ride, and the cost of the probation that had to be paid every month was somehow taken care of. During this discussion, Billy told Jim Gray that it was his marijuana the police found in the car and Mitch had taken the blame for Billy. That sounded like something Mitch would do.

Mr. Long was free to go, and his lawyer, Skip, told the newspapers that it was an old law in Texas that you could shoot someone if you thought there was a threat to yourself. There was never any mention of such a law at the trial; it was just something that he thought of later. Jim was outraged and swore to himself that Long would pay, and the jury too, if he could arrange it.

CHAPTER 16

The return to Maryland was anything but happy. Earl Long was free, and Becky was unable to understand how it could be true. Even explaining it to friends and relatives was difficult because it did not make sense that a man could chase down two boys and shoot them yet be found not guilty.

The broken family moved from Maryland to Michigan in 1988, after West Mark Medical purchased Tracor and it was decided to close Medinautics. They lived in a great area called Brighton, which was about forty-five minutes from Jim's work in Wixom, Michigan. The new house in Brighton was ready just about the time school started, but there were no children in the house. The sting of Long's trial weighed heavily on them, so a plan was formulated in Jim's mind to kill Earl Long, who was living free in Houston. Plane tickets and credit card receipts would leave a trail of evidence for a trip to Houston. Traveling with any kind of weapon would also pose a problem for airplane travel, and no one should know that he was out of town. Money was still tight after the move and purchase of a house, so he could only plan on a drive down to Houston using cash for gas and meals. It would take about twenty-four hours each way to drive, so there had to be enough time that could be covered with a good story. There would also have to be a little time for sleep if driving straight through both directions.

Some years before, Jim had a chance to buy a .357 Dan Wesson revolver for only $100. There was no record of the transaction, and the pistol was not registered in any way that could be traced through the previous owners. Jim Gray loaded the weapon with six .357 Magnum shells and planned how he could leave work early the day of the trip and drive straight through to Houston. He had made such a trip before when the family drove straight through after being told about Mitch's death. After arriving at work early as usual, Jim complained about feeling sick and would have to go back home. Instead of heading home, Jim Gray headed south on I-275 out of Novi/Farmington to connect to I-75 and drive past Toledo, Ohio, to Cincinnati. Crossing Kentucky, Tennessee, and Arkansas into Texas, he arrived in Houston early on Friday morning and watched as Bonnie Long left the house. She was probably taking a trip to the store or going to work. Jim was counting on catching Earl Sr. alone but was prepared to take out both Earl and Bonnie if needed. The scenario would be that Earl killed Bonnie and then turned the gun on himself, but now it seemed that the plan was much simpler. He would shoot Earl with the untraceable handgun and make it look like a suicide. With Long's police record and known rash actions, it sounded like it would be believable in Jim's mind.

Mitch's father slipped the pistol in his belt near the small of his back so that it could not be seen when Long answered the door. He pulled a ball cap down over his eyes and picked up a small pizza box left over from a meal he had during the long drive to Houston. Approaching the front door, Mr. Gray tried the doorbell and also knocked on the door to be sure Earl could hear it. When Earl opened the door, Jim explained that Mrs. Long had ordered a pizza for lunch and the charge would be $8.95 cash. Earl grumbled about how that was the dumbest thing he had ever heard of but turned to get his wallet from someplace within the house. Mitch's father quickly moved into the house and met Earl returning from another room with his wallet. He shoved the gun barrel into Earl's open mouth as he announced, "This is for Mitch, you son of a bitch." One shot through the brain was all it took from the very loud .357 magnum handgun.

The house was very quiet as Mitch's father carefully took the wallet from Earl's hand and replaced it with the handgun. Earl was dressed in a pair of jeans and a T-shirt with writing on it. Jim slid the wallet into one of Earl's back pockets and moved to the door. Surveying the room, it looked as if Earl had walked into the living room and shot himself for reasons that Bonnie and others could explain to the police. *Poor Earl was out of work, depressed about the trial, or just plain crazy,* Jim rationalized to himself. It did not matter to Jim how they explained why the man killed himself.

The family received a call from Joe Magnum, the Assistant DA in Houston, on Valentine's Day 1989 to let them know that Long had shot himself, maybe on purpose or by accident. The main thing was that Long had gone to his just reward, and the assistant district attorney was glad it had ended that way.

CHAPTER 17

Jim and Becky purchased an old farm outside of Woodville, Texas, during the time the Carsons, Becky's parents, were in their senior years. They planned to fix up the old farmhouse that was over one hundred years old and in bad shape. There was a pasture to the north and a pasture to the south of the farmhouse, and the rest of the property was heavily wooded and showed evidence of former generations. The Carsons lived in a house they built on some ancestral property near the old farm, and Jim could walk around investigating signs of past generations.

Even after the announcement about Earl Long being dead, what was left of the family did not heal as it should. Becky and Jim had problems with intimacy and the loving-kindness that had existed before the ordeal of losing Mitch, the trial of Earl Long Sr., and the true story of his demise. Things just were not the same anymore. Jim began to stay out late with friends from work while Becky became bitter and demanding.

They were drifting apart, and they were 1,500 miles away from their home in Texas. Jim's work forced him to spend long hours at the lab while Becky reached the end of her patience. She decided to go back to Texas and help with her ailing mother. Her dad was getting up in age, and the work was too much for him. The weeks turned into months and the months into years as Jim and Becky lost all but minimal communication. Becky packed the black Chevrolet blazer with her personal things and headed toward Woodville to see if she could help. The house was a three bedroom, two-bath frame structure secluded in the East Texas piney woods. A long driveway through the woods led to the two acres where the cozy house was located. When her mom was in good health, the yard was beautiful with natural landscaping of azaleas, bridal wreath, and magnolias that bloomed part of the year. The dogwood trees and crape myrtle were scattered around the property, along with pear trees and a large fig bush in the backyard. Her roses grew along the single-car garage up to the door of the small office and a canning room used by Becky's mom and dad in earlier years. She missed Jim terribly and longed to have the love and family that had been lost.

In happier times, Jim, Mitch, and Becky visited the Carsons for weekends and holidays. Sometimes they had cookouts or a wiener roasts over a small bonfire in the yard behind the garage. They would sit in lawn chairs and talk until dark while enjoying the surrounding beauty or sipping a mint julep made from the plants growing in the rose beds. Becky's dad, PaPa, would entertain with his stories of the old days or pursue some activity with little Mitch until his bath and bedtime. Those were good times that provided great memories, but times had changed. Mitch was gone, and Jim was immersed in his work, which left Becky alone at home with no one to comfort her. Now that Becky's mother was down with bad knees, overweight, and had Alzheimer's, she was needed in Woodville. Her dad was approaching ninety years of age and could not lift his wife from the bed to the chair, but he would try anyway. Becky took over the lifting, cleaning, cooking, and the misery that had settled into the once-happy retirement home. She cared for her aging parents for what seemed like an eternity and tried not to go completely crazy. By the time her mother died, she was exhausted but continued to help her dad cope with losing her mother until he died two years later.

Her brother, Gary, had pestered their dad until he signed over the property and his money to him and had given him power of attorney. Becky was left with nothing, and she did not have the strength to carry on. She died on a Saturday morning and was found by her brother, Gary, later that day, still sitting in her mom's old rocking chair. The television was playing an old western movie that she had probably seen numerous times but still loved from her childhood. She died alone with no one to care for her. She died of a broken heart.

Gary stripped the house of anything of value. He took the old grandfather clock promised to Becky, heirloom quilts, cash, guns, and items that belonged to Mitch and Jim that were in the house.

Jim was notified by Becky's relatives that she had passed, but Jim could not leave the present experiment long enough to make the trip to Texas for the funeral. Becky was laid to rest in the local cemetery next to Mitch, her mother, and her dad. Mount Pisgah Cemetery is located just off of the country road that runs by the Carson property. By the time Jim was able to get to Woodville, months had passed. During that time, Carson relatives had taken anything of value from the house and had claimed all of the property and the money from PaPa's checking accounts. The only thing left for Jim in the piney woods of East Texas was an old farm that he and Becky had purchased to go with the land her father had promised to her. The land she was promised went to Gary. Jim visited the cemetery where Becky and Mitch were placed and sat on the little concrete bench that faced the Carson headstone. He had brought artificial flowers for Becky and some small Corvettes for Mitch, knowing it would be some time before he could return. After a good cry for the way things had turned out, he drove his fairly new Chevrolet pick-up to the farm property and unlocked the gate to the wooded drive that led to the old house. It was rundown and barely livable, but sitting on the old rotting porch, he felt at home. It was good to be back in Texas, and if only he could have his family back, things would be great.

CHAPTER 18

Jim had a recurring feeling that he needed revenge on those who stole from Becky and her parents. Gary had taken over part of the Carson land and eventually gained deed to about forty acres that were originally used for their first "camp," as they called it. Mr. Carson purchased a nice mobile home and set it up for weekend use while he and Mrs. Carson lived in Houston. Additional land came up for sale that adjoined the original purchases, so a house was built on a two-acre tract in anticipation of retirement. Gary and his second wife took over the mobile home after he had become involved in a thief scheme in Port Arthur. Gary worked for the Gulf States Utilities Company, which was the electric supplier for the golden triangle area, and he stole copper wire to sell at a scrap yard called Port Iron Works but was not smart enough to withhold his name as the seller. He was charged with theft and was about to go to trial when Mr. Carson influenced the judge to let him move to Woodville to run his own business. The business purchased by Mr. Carson for Gary was a butane delivery service that included a large storage tank and gas delivery truck. This kept Gary out of prison and enabled him to take over the mobile home and land around it.

Years later, when Mrs. Carson was gone and Mr. Carson was in a weakened condition, Gary cajoled him to sign over the rest of the land and house that had been promised to Becky. The thieving, lying ways of this brother-in-law put Jim into a rage every time he thought about it, and it was one of those times.

There was an old 303 Enfield bolt-action rifle that Jim had purchased while in college still stored in the old farmhouse. Several guys in the dormitory had purchased that type of rifle at the local Sears & Roebuck store for fifteen dollars each back in 1961. Also available with the rifles were full metal jackets as well as lead nose ammunition. Jim had purchased both types of shells to use for target practice those many years ago and still had most of them hidden in the small closet of the front bedroom. A plan was formulated to take away Gary's ill-gotten gains and exact revenge on the one who added to Becky's depression before she died. Jim was ready to return to Michigan and had not interacted with anyone in the area. Having driven down just to see Becky's gravesite and check on the remote farm property, he had not let anyone know exactly where he was going. He had paid cash for a few supplies he would need, such as drinks, bread, and sandwich meat, so there were no records of the purchases. He had enough gas in the truck to make it out of the state, and he planned to slip out of town unnoticed.

The plan was to catch Gary as he left for work the next morning and take one quick shot to end the miserable feeling he had about how Becky had been cheated out of her inheritance. Jim retrieved the old gun from the closet and checked it over, along with the ammunition. He chose to use the lead-tipped shells so the possibility that the shooting could be attributed to a deer hunter who missed and hit Gary while he was driving to work. *It could work,* Jim thought. Before daybreak, Jim cleaned up any evidence of him being at the old farmhouse and left the property to take his place on the road that Gary would use. He had some time to wait, so he went to the cemetery one more time to be with Becky and Mitch. About an hour before Gary would drive by Bounds Road, Jim parked his pick-up truck at a point where he could get a good shot at anyone driving down Seneca Road. At 7:50 a.m., Jim could see the old Chevrolet truck that Gary drove to work every day, and Jim turned in the driver's seat so he could aim the old rifle accurately. When Jim could see his face, he squeezed off a shot that zapped through the windshield and hit the cheating, lying bastard in the upper chest. The old truck served off the road and into a barbed wire fence that ran along Seneca Road. Jim swiveled back into driving position and laid the gun so that it could not be seen by other drivers as he started his truck and eased down Bounds Road toward Highway 190. He wanted to drive fast and get out of there but restrained himself so that no accident or unwanted attention would get him caught in the area. He turned onto Highway 190 and headed toward Jasper before deciding that he wanted to get rid of the rifle and ammunition permanently. When he crossed the bridge over Dam Bee Reservoir, Jim slowed long enough to launch the rifle over the rail and into the deep water, and then he threw the boxes of shells into the water after it. At that point, he had made the shot, slipped away unnoticed, and disposed of the incriminating evidence.

CHAPTER 19

Jim returned to Michigan and to the research lab he had devoted himself to for the last ten years. The work included experiments on comatose subjects who had been dismissed as no longer having any hope of returning to the world. The ideas that were being tried on the patients had started with lab animals and brain-dead subjects. By isolating the life force of the subject, the scientists were able to separate the spirit from the body. The spirit of the subject could be held outside the body for a couple of hours and then placed back into it. The spirit was electrically removed and held in a glass chamber for observation. It had the form of the subject but very little, if any, substance. It appeared to be a ghost or a vapor in its confinement. At first, using small animals, the spirit looked like a projection of the original subject and would move around like the animal would have done if not in a comatose condition. When the spirit was returned to the subject, the animal could be revived and function normally again. Years of experimentation and documentation led to the first comatose accident victim. The patient was brain-dead, and the family had given up hope of recovery. The research team and technicians constructed a larger chamber to hold the spirit, which might be extracted from the subject. It included observation windows and climate control in anticipation of the time that such an opportunity to experiment on a human subject became available. The larger chamber was designed to function the same way as the prototype used on laboratory animals with little variation. The power ratio was increased proportionally to the prototype equipment, and the chamber was ready when the news came that a subject was going to be available.

In the sterile conditions in the laboratory, the subject was prepared for spirit separation, and all the monitoring equipment was connected. The readouts were as predicted: no brain activity and no vital signs. The nodes placed on the subject were reconnected to a current that was to be used to remove the spirit, if any remained in the comatose patient. A vapor began to form in the observation chamber. Then a human shape evolved that could be recognized as the comatose subject, and the mouth formed words that were at first too soft to hear without amplification. The chamber's sound recording equipment helped the team understand the monologue and could provide for any two-way communication. The ghostly form said, "I am the spirit of Henry Atkins, and I stay with my body until it dies and then I can be free." He further said, "My spirit will then be able to move through time and space for eternity." Before any team member could attempt to communicate, the spirit disappeared from the chamber and did not seem to have gone back into the subject. Other attempts to separate the vapor that called itself Henry's Spirit from the body failed. They worked around the clock trying to duplicate the event, but no spirit appeared, and the patient continued in the comatose condition, being kept alive by machines that did his breathing and provided blood circulation. The afternoon of the next day, the team voted to remove Henry Atkins from life support and return the body to the family for burial.

The research team did not fully understand the results of the first experiment with a human subject but saw great potential in freeing a person's spirit to move through time and space. The project scientist claimed their experiment to be a success.

CHAPTER 20

With the reported success of the first human subject came better funding for additional equipment and laboratory space. The size of the team grew, and Jim carefully selected those who thought as he did. He made it a point to become friends with each of them. He had a haunting feeling that somehow their research could be used to change his life for the better. There was limited success with comatose subjects. It seemed that if they were atheist, there was one spirit to be found. Christian subjects had two spirits; one was identified as the Holy Ghost, and it refused to leave the body until death. One subject who was in a coma showed some brain activity when connected to the monitors and nodes. This subject had a spirit that was extractable, and the team confirmed through interviews with the ghostly aberration in the chamber that the human spirit was only held back by the body. Once released from the body, the spirit could move where it wanted and when it wanted. During the spirits' absence from the body, the subjects are virtually dead but revive when the spirits return. The subject was a woman named June Tangelo, and her spirit disappeared for a short time and then returned to the chamber. Her spirit said, "I have traveled through time and space to see myself and family in years past." The science team tried to ask her many questions, but she told them that she was free and wanted to stay that way. She disappeared and did not return, leaving her body without any sign of life.

Everyone on the team wanted to experiment with a normal person but was overruled by the management group. The danger was too great and the liability extreme, so Jim began to plan his own experiment aided by the close associates he had developed. Each of the RX7-Team, as they called themselves, knew their job well and realized the chances that they were taking. The management group decided to move the laboratory to Houston and into a new facility provided by the Herman Memorial Foundation. Specific goals were set for the experiments, and additional funding was provided. It was an excellent time to do a clandestine experiment while the equipment was being moved and tested. Jim was the first volunteer for the procedure of extracting his spirit. They had learned from the previous subjects that the spirit can only remain outside the body for four hours, and then it fades away or does not return to the chamber. Jim knew exactly where and when he wanted to go. The time was February 28, 1986, and the place was the apartments where Mitch lived back then. If only the spirit could accomplish the trip and get back for reinsertion in the waiting body…It was most important that he try, and if it failed, he did not care anymore.

CHAPTER 21

The group called the RX7-Team met secretly to plan the experiment, as dictated by Jim Gray. He and a few others set up the equipment and laboratory for the spirit-extraction attempt to take place that night at midnight. The usual employees would not be around to question the clandestine activities, and the guards were not suspicious of the group working late into the night. Jim had spent most of the last ten years working on the details needed to help comatose patients and the spirit removal that had come as a side effect of the true goal of reviving a subject on whom everyone had given up hope. Jim prepared himself physically and mentally for the endeavor by praying to God and spending time in meditation. He wanted to get the mission clearly in his mind and not be tempted to run free or fail to return, as he had seen others do.

The team connected all of the monitoring and extraction devices to Jim's body and head. It was a few minutes after midnight when the power was applied for the extraction, and a faint figure began to form in the chamber. He could only whisper to the team, "I will be back," as he disappeared from their view. Jim was on his way back in time by willing the movement in time and space. He willed himself to find Mitch in Houston on February 28, 1986, and stopped inside a gated apartment complex named Smiling Wood Apartments, where Mitch had lived, and he wanted to be there to find him sometime before nightfall. Jim walked around the deserted complex and encountered a little girl playing with her doll on some apartment steps. She could see Jim, even though he was little more than a man made from smoke. She asked, "Mister, what are you doing here?" Jim answered by saying, "I am looking for a boy named Mitch." The pretty little girl, who Jim guessed was around six years old, was excited as he described the tall man who had become her friend. She said, "I know him; he stops and talks to me, and I like him." She said, "He is the only person that will sit with me and listen to what I have to say." Jim asked her, "Please don't tell anyone that you have seen me," as he turned and proceeded toward Mitch's apartment.

Jim had been thinking about how he could reach Mitch and what to tell him that would avoid the shooting tonight. Then he saw Mitch leaving his apartment and walking to the pay phone near the apartment office. He listened when Mitch told the person on the other end that he would not be able to work tonight because his car would not start. That was probably why Mitch had been at home that evening when Billy came by his apartment. The chain of events would lead to the death of Mitch and the critical wound in Billy's neck.

Jim followed him back to the apartment and slipped in behind him without being noticed. Maybe it was the bright sunlight or that Mitch was depressed about his car, but Mitch did not see him outside, and now they could talk without others seeing or hearing. The first thing Jim said to him was, "Mitch, don't be afraid. I need to talk to you." Startled but attentive, Mitch listened to his dad explain about being in spirit form and that he had traveled from the future. The main thing he wanted to relate to Mitch was that he was in danger and something had to be done. Jim said, "Mitch, some bad things are about to happen so we must leave the apartments."

Mitch replied, "Dad, my car will not start and it will be hard to go anywhere." Jim said, "I know how to fix the problem on your car."

When the family came to Houston after Mitch was killed, the car was taken to a shop for repair. It turned out to be the key switch that was bad, and it could be easily bypassed, as Jim knew from his car-stealing experience as a boy. Jim and Becky had to clean out the apartment on that sad trip, so he knew that Mitch had money stashed in his drawer.

Jim said, "Get the tools that I gave you and the money that you have in your drawer so we can get out of here before Billy arrives."

"How do you know that Billy is coming over?" asked Mitch.

"This has all happened before. I will explain further as we travel," his dad said.

The red 1967 Firebird was parked in the lot near Mitch's apartment, and Jim explained to him how to bypass the key switch to make the engine start. The exhaust pipes soon rumbled as the big Pontiac V-8 engine came to life.

CHAPTER 22

Mitch pulled out of the parking space at the Smiling Wood Apartment and headed to the security gates as his dad instructed. Jim noticed a young man and a couple of women near Mitch's apartment who were unloading items from a Mazda pickup truck and realized that the time for Billy to arrive was drawing near.

"Son," Jim said, "the safest thing I can come up with is a drive to Woodville." He told Mitch that the whole story would be related to him as they made the two-hour drive, but it dawned on Jim that there might be things better not discussed at this time.

Turning on Gulf Bank Road, Mitch headed to Highway 59 for the trip north to Livingston, then a right turn to Woodville on Highway 190. Jim began to tell the strange story of why he was there in a spirit form with a few interruptions to answers questions from Mitch. He said, "Billy will be arriving at the apartment complex around dark and he will run into his brother-in-law." "There will be words exchanged with Earl Jr. who is Lori's brother and then you and Billy will leave the apartments." Jim then told him, "A stranger will chase you and even shoot at Billy's car, so that is why the trip out of town is necessary." Jim tried to stay with the heart of the story, but if Mitch thought his friend was going to be hurt, he would have turned around and made an attempt to save Billy. Mitch asked, "Why did the man come after us?" and Jim explained, "Billy's wife, Lori, is the reason. Earl Long Jr. is moving into your apartment complex today and when Billy sees him, they have harsh words. The little coward calls his dad and Earl Sr. jumps into his car and comes after Billy. Even though he has never met Billy, he hates him because he and Lori were married without her dad's permission."

"Billy and his father-in-law have spoken on the phone at least once, but that ended in a verbal fight according to the information that I have," Jim told Mitch.

The ride was long enough to allow Jim to explain a little about the technology that enabled the trip through time and space. He also said it took many years of research and experimentation to discover these phenomena and there were still many unknowns about the consequences of this trip.

Mitch entered the city limits of Woodville and asked Jim, "Can we stop to get something to eat? Jim replied, "Let's continue to your grandparents' house so that no one will see us and to avoid some unexpected thing that might happen if we stop." They drove onto the driveway that led to the Carson's house and Jim directed him, "drive part of the way down the wooded drive and stop so we can talk some more." Mitch listened to the explanation of the RX7-Team project, and

Jim told him, "The name was suggested because the car that Mr. Long was driving was a Mazda RX-7."

"Dad," Mitch asked, "Do you remember the drawing I made for the art contest that had a bull skull and Indian symbols?" Jim replied, "I remember the drawing, and I think it was very good how you made up the picture using small ink dots." During the discussion, Mitch said, "I named the drawing *Time Shift* because I had the feeling it represented a move through time and space." Then he said, "Your project sounds like a time shift." Jim agreed, saying, "That makes sense to me." Jim thought that Mitch was in a safe place for that night in 1986, with his grandparents nearby and about two hours' distance from the place where he would have been killed. Jim prepared himself for the trip to the chamber and faded away as he told Mitch, "I love you, son. You must be strong."

CHAPTER 23

Upon return to the laboratory chamber, Jim's spirit entered back into his body. The urge to join with the Supreme Spirit Being was overcome, and the desire to be free of the body was resisted. The RX7-Team members did their job well, and Jim was awake and talking to them in a matter of minutes. Some of the first words Jim said to the team were, "Let's call this procedure Time Shift," and he thanked each member of the team for their excellent work.

Jim was in a daze as he walked to the parking garage and started his old Chevrolet truck for the trip home. Instead of going to the apartment he had leased since returning to Houston, he had a strong urge to drive to Woodville and stay at the old farm for a few days. He knew there was some sort of experiment in the lab that he was deeply involved in it, but his full memory had not yet returned. His old truck was where he had left it in the parking lot, but something seemed to be different. He had stopped caring about keeping the truck clean, but now it was much cleaner than he remembered and had new tires and looked like it had been waxed. He felt a little better by the time he drove into the long dirt driveway to the farm. He stopped to unlock the gate that led to the farmhouse and then continued down the drive with dense forest on either side. When he came to the clearing where the old farmhouse stood, he was shocked to see how good it looked. It had good paint, the old sagging porch was now like new, and the yard was well kept with a white fence and flowers. Jim could not believe his eyes when the front door of the old house opened and Becky stepped out on the porch with a smile and a wave.

He ran to her and hugged her as if he had not seen her in many years, and Becky expressed a little surprise when she said, "Well, that was a great hug…" but her mouth was covered by Jim's kisses as he apologized for all the things he had done wrong. Jim prayed to God right then and there to forgive him for the sins that he had committed in a different time. She did not know what he meant but was thrilled to have him home and in such a good mood.

They made their way into the living room where a fire invited them to sit and enjoy the warmth and comfort. Becky reminded Jim, "The kids will be arriving shortly to stay over the weekend, and I have everything ready." The memories continued to flood Jim's brain, and some of the details started to make sense as he took time to analyze it.

By going back and saving Mitch from the murderous Earl Long, the wasted years, heartaches, and depression were like a nightmare, and Jim felt as though he were coming out of a long sleep. Joy and peace filled Jim's soul as he realized that the kids who Becky was expecting where Mitch, Tess, and their children. Tess had two older girls, but there were two boys named Stephen and Michael, who would also be bringing their families with them. Mitch did not die that night in February, Jim remembered; he married and provided grandchildren for Jim and Becky. *Family*... now there was an encouraging word for Jim, who had spent lonely years in rage, acts of revenge, and the heavy feeling of loss. Immersed in his work, he had found a way to save Mitch and gain his life back. He thanked God for allowing it all to happen and for giving him a second chance to enjoy life.

The travel through time and space had restored a new life to the family, and there would be no need to do that again... Or would there?

EPILOGUE

The three kids in the Mustang were cornered at a liquor store trying to call for the police when Billy was shot and killed. Earl Long was arrested at the scene, taken to jail, and charged with murder. When his trial came up a year later, Mr. Long was found guilty. The jury believed the witnesses to the shooting, and he was sent to prison to serve his sentence. As predicted by the assistant district attorney, he did not last long in prison with his attitude. He was found dead in the prison showers a few months after the trial.

Mitch entered art school and developed his skills as an artist and illustrator. His original ideas and way-out drawings attracted the attention of rock bands, movie animators, and commercial producers. He married his high school friend, Tess, and they raised her two girls with the two boys they had over the next few years. Mitch had always enjoyed the woods, so he brought the family to the Gray farm in Woodville on weekends and holidays, to the delight of Jim and

Becky Gray. Mitch had a special tree in the woods where his dad had helped him carve his initials as a boy. Mitch took his sons to the tree when they were old enough and helped them add their initials to the bark.

Jim Gray continued to work at the Herman Memorial Research facility, but only as a consultant on special cases. He retired to the farm in Woodville to live to an old age while enjoying his children, grandchildren, and great-grandchildren. He kept tract of any progress on the Time Shift procedures…just in case.

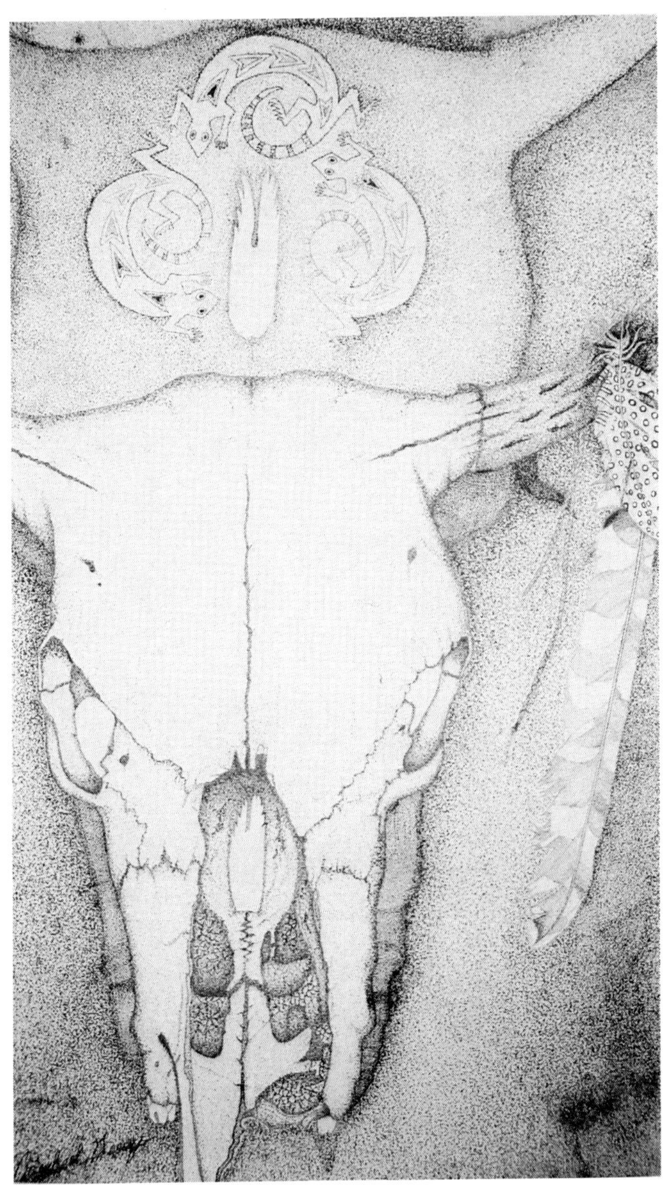

CHAPTER 1

Her name was Maude Moneypenny, and she was a young Cherokee girl who lived in a household in Holdenville, Oklahoma. The city was the county seat in Hughes County having about 75 percent white people and 15 percent Native Americans. The Cherokee are a people native to North America who, at the time of European contact in the sixteenth century, inhabited what is now the eastern and southeastern United States. Most were forcibly moved westward to the Ozark Plateau in the 1830s and are one of the groups rcferred to as the Five Civilized Tribes. They refer to themselves as *Tsa-la-gi* or *Sa lah gi* with a literal translation of "principal people." The characteristics of the Cherokee people were described in the writings of William Bartram in his journey through their land in 1776:

> The Cherokee are tall, erect and moderately robust; their limbs well shaped, so as generally to form a perfect human figure; their features regular

> and countenance open, dignified and placid, yet the forehead and brow are so formed as to strike you instantly with heroism and bravery; their eyes, though rather small yet active and full of fire, the iris is always black and the nose is commonly inclining to the aquiline. Their countenance and actions exhibit an air of magnanimity, superiority and independence. Their complexion is reddish brown or copper color; their hair, long, lank, coarse, and black as a raven and reflecting the like luster at different exposures to the light. The women of the Cherokees are tall, slender, erect, and of a delicate frame; their features formed with perfect symmetry; the countenance cheerful and friendly; and they move with a becoming grace and dignity.

As a young girl, Maude's parents migrated to Oklahoma and found a family that not only befriend them but also helped them become established in the community. Maude was twenty-one years old when the 1900 census was taken, and she had completed her public school education in a small school down the road from the house where she lived. Her parents had let her live with the Anderson family so she could learn from the white people and go to an English-speaking school. Her Indian family was poor, as many of her people were who lived in the Indian Nation. Only Indians could own land in Oklahoma at that time, but it did not do them much good. They did not have enough money to buy land and pay the property taxes.

Maude met a boy in school named Thomas Gray, and they became friends. The Andersons did not mind if her friend Thomas came by their house to visit with Maude after she had finished the household chores that earned her keep, so the friendship developed into love during and after their school years. Thomas Gray and Maude were married and started a family in 1897. Thomas's family owned a farm in Iowa before they migrated to Oklahoma, so when he and Maude were married, his dad could buy land in Oklahoma in her name, and it provided a home for the newlyweds. That worked out well for a while, but Thomas was not happy being a farmer and longed to continue the migration southward. He and Maude moved to Camden, Arkansas, with their sons, Everett, Aubrey, and a baby named Louie. Little Louie came along in 1908 before the family became settled in Camden, Arkansas.

By the time Louie was thirteen years old, his dad, Thomas Jefferson Gray, left the family behind and went in search of another home. The idea was for Tom, as he was called, to get work and continue to support the family. With times being hard, there was little work, so Tom found himself at a soup kitchen in downtown Birmingham, Alabama, on a cold day in 1921. A group of church members were arriving early to begin cooking for the noon meal, and Tom helped them carry in the groceries. The building was across from an old Methodist church, and Tom happened to be a Methodist. The guys entering the mission kitchen asked Tom if he would like to help them prepare the meal and then go with them to the church across the street before they began to serve the homeless people that came after noon. Tom jumped at the chance to cook, serve, and eat. The group church members provided four or five hams, bunches of carrots, a sack of onions, stalks of celery, and each person was assigned a job to do. A large stainless steel pot about the size of a kettledrum was already on an open flame in the middle of the large kitchen. It was about half full of white navy beans and must have been boiling for hours. The hams were cut into small pieces, and all the meat, fat, and bones were thrown into the pot. Tom was assigned the task of cutting up celery, onions, and carrots along with some other men. When he asked about washing the carrots and scraping the outside, he was told by one of the leaders, "Cut 'em up and throw 'em in."

The onions were peeled, but that was the only produce processed before being cut up and placed into the pot along with salt and pepper. Tom was introduced to a little ceremony that the kitchen workers performed when the soup was cooking. They passed the cigars around to each man and lit them. After a few puffs, each guy flicked some ashes into the big soup pot and told Tom that was the finish for the Homeless Soup preparation.

With that out of the way, several large sticks of baloney and about a dozen loaves of white bread appeared. The baloney was sliced, and one piece was placed on two pieces of bread with a little mayonnaise; it was wrapped individually so it would be ready to hand out later. Around ten thirty a.m., most of the work was done and some of the crew wanted to go to the church service across the street. Tom went with them and entered the large decorative sanctuary of the old Methodist church to sit with the guys he had met while working in the kitchen. Tom wrote down the recipe for the soup and tried to imagine enough for his family back in Arkansas.

CHAPTER 2

Louie Gray stood on the train platform that January morning in 1924. His bright blue eyes were carefully studying each board of the platform and each nail that fastened the underlying structure. His black wavy hair was covered with a boy's-style cap, and his ears stuck out a little farther than usual. Someone would later describe Louie as a Clark Gable lookalike, right down to the dimples in his cheeks. It was only a few days until his fourteenth birthday, and he wanted to go home to his mother. He left home three months before Christmas because his mom had taken up with a man named Oliver. Mr. Oliver was all right, but Louie missed his dad, Thomas Gray, who had left his mother to move to Bessemer, Alabama, almost a year ago. He did not know if there had been a divorce or just a breakup. His mother was full-blooded Cherokee Indian, so he was not sure they had ever officially gotten married. He had an older brother who had left for California about the time his dad moved out, which left him feeling lonely and unwanted. He had been able to find odd jobs to provide enough food for himself and was able to sleep almost anywhere near the places he worked. Now, a decision had to be made.

Louie telegraphed his mom the day before, and he was waiting near the telegraph office to see if he would get on the train for home or if he would strike out to California to find his brother Everett. As he waited on the cold platform, he contemplated his choices. If his mom telegraphed that she would welcome him home, he would catch the ten thirty a.m. train to Shreveport, Louisiana, but if no word came by that time or if the answer was not to his liking, he would start the westward trip. Sitting alone on a wooden bench that was at one end of the platform, he became aware of a figure standing near him. He could make out that it was a man, but it was more ghostly than flesh and began to speak in a soft tone to the wayward boy.

"Louie," said the man. The boy looked at him intensely as the man continued, "I know you are trying to make a decision, and I have come to help you." "My name is not important now, but I will tell you someday, if you can believe me." He waited for the boy to answer.

"I will listen to what you have to say," Louie said.

"Go back home and stay with your mom and Mr. Oliver for a few more years." Then he said, "There is a family named Terrell where you will find friends and a girl named Annette, who will be important to you for the rest of your life. Don't forget what I have told you, and don't share it with anyone," the ghostly figure said before fading away.

Louie was still sitting on the platform, pondering what the transparent man had told him when the telegraph operator stuck his head out of a small window in the building that served the train platform and said, "Hey, are you Louie Gray?"

The boy ran to the window and told the telegraph man, "I'm Louie Gray." The man handed a telegram to Louie, along with a twenty-dollar bill. The message said,

> Louie Gray—stop
>
> Please come home on next train—stop
>
> Have wired $20—stop
>
> We will meet train—stop
>
> Mom—stop

Those were beautiful words to Louie, and he immediately purchased a ticket on the ten-thirty-morning train to Shreveport. Upon arriving at the Shreveport train station, his mom and Mr. Oliver met him with a big hug and a cheerful welcome. His mom was dressed in a white blouse, a full black skirt, and wore a large brimmed hat. She looked great. Mr. Oliver looked sharp in a dark business suit as he escorted the small party to his large open car for the trip to their house. Maude's olive complexion did not betray her Indian heritage but only gave her more appeal, if that were possible. Louie told them about his adventures during the last few months and then asked, "Do you know a family named Terrell?"

CHAPTER 3

Annette was the thirteenth child of Mr. and Mrs. Terrell who had a farm outside Cedar Grove, Louisiana, near Shreveport. Even at that gangly age, Annette was a beautiful young lady. She was tall and lanky but could run with her older brothers through the woods and fields. Her dad, Isaac Terrell, died in 1908 and was buried in the little family cemetery on the farm only a year after little Annette was born. Her mother, Annie Terrell, was a hard-shelled little lady, as she had to be to raise a large family on the meager income from the farm. Annette had seven brothers and five sisters, so she was a special little girl around the farm, and even the farm hands paid extra attention to her. She was strong and lean from trying to keep up with her brothers and helping with the chores around the house.

One day while tagging along after her brothers, she noticed a new boy had joined the group by the name of Louie Gray. They were about the same age, which made them younger than the other children. There was an attraction between them, and they became good friends as they walked the fields or sat on the old farmhouse porch together. Louie was a tough kid who would not let anyone pick on Annette and never backed down from a challenge, no matter how big the other kid was. He did not talk much about his family and the move from Camden, Arkansas to Shreveport with his mother. Annette told him what she knew of her dad, aunts, and uncles to keep the conversations going.

They walked to school together and studied reading, writing, and arithmetic in the small school building near Cedar Grove. Annette's brothers would go with them sometimes, but they often ran off to find adventure at the swimming hole or in the woods. Louie was interested in school and was a natural at arithmetic, but he mainly wanted to make sure that Annette was escorted every morning.

The decision made at the train station had brought him back home to meet Annette, and they were together as children for almost two years before Louie decided to join the army and see the world. He was not quite sixteen, which was the minimum age for joining, so he lied about his age to enlist in the infantry division of the US Army. He took his basic training at Fort Sam Houston in San Antonio, Texas, and became a gunnery sergeant after a few years. During that time, he wrote to Annette and assured her that he would return for her. On leave from the army one time, he was able to travel to Birmingham, Alabama, to see his dad, Thomas Jefferson Gray, who had a barbershop near town. He had married a lady from Bessemer, Alabama, after leaving Maude in Arkansas, a few years before. It was a chance meeting, even though Louie knew a little about his dad's location, when he saw a man walking down the street that looked just like him. It turned out that Louie and his dad had a close resemblance that anyone could see. Both of them had black wavy hair, dimples in their cheeks when they smiled, and their ears stuck out like Clark Gable's did. He had a good visit with his dad, and neither one of them tried to place blame for what had happened to separate a father from his son when Thomas Gray left Arkansas.

CHAPTER 4

About the time Louie met Annette, her mother and two brothers lived on the farm known as the Terrell Plantation in south Shreveport (Cedar Groves), Louisiana. Later, her brothers were away from home often, so it left Annette and her mother alone during a time of unrest among the white and black people. It became dangerous for two women to be alone, and one of the hired colored men named Enoch Arthur was very uneasy about the ladies because Annette was about fifteen years old and her mother was ill quite a bit. He would come to the tool house for plows or things needed to work because he was afraid that some of the young Negroes would harm Annette if he sent them for tools. After a while, Enoch told her mother, "You and the girl are in danger by staying here by yourselves." Annette's mother did not believe him at first, so Enoch talked to one of her sons. Her brother begged Annette by saying, "Go to town and stay with our older sister." Annette took the good advice and moved to Shreveport to stay with her older sister.

Annette had a friend named Nellie Duncan who was sixteen years old and had a job at the telephone office. She talked Annette into going to the telephone office to apply for a job too. The following morning, she went with her, and while talking to the chief operator, Annette told her, "I am sixteen years old." The chief operator questioned her further because she knew better. When Annette told her the correct age, she told Annette that there were no child labor laws and a birth certificate was not required to get the job. She said, "I will give you a chance by signing you up for a class of twenty-five people that is starting tomorrow morning."

Only seventeen people finished the course, and Annette was the only one to make a hundred on the test. The telephone operator supervisor hired Annette, and she worked all the years that Louie was away discovering America. She waited for each letter from him and longed for the day that he would return to her as he had promised. She wrote to Louie most every day and told him all the details that she knew about her family and about her work life. The letters included how she was born in Shreveport in 1908 and what she had been told about her father, Isaac Nathaniel Terrell, who died when she was a baby. She wrote about her mother, Caroline Annette Raimond Terrell, and her way of getting what she wanted by faking ill health, saying, "I'll be dead soon and you can go then."

Annette wanted Louie to know everything about her, so she related that she was the thirteenth child and her father had died of pneumonia caused by trying to save his crops from the flood of the Red River when the banks gave away, which resulted in great loss to many farmers. He left Annette's mother and ten of the thirteen children on a large farm that her mother tried to manage, but due to her ill health she finally had to lease out most of the land to others. That brought in enough money with the crops that they lived very comfortably until the older children began to leave home. One brother went to war, and the sisters got married one at a time until it was only Annette's two young brothers, mother, and her left on the farm. They walked four miles to school, but sometimes the brothers would play hooky and she had to go to school alone. They finally quit school altogether, and she had to walk alone much of the time. Annette would run most of the way to school because she was afraid of what the hired hand had told her mother. That is why she quit school at fifteen years old and went to work at the telephone company.

After a while, her mother sold the farm and moved to town, which was named Cedar Groves and later became south Shreveport, Louisiana. Her childhood was not unhappy, but she missed so many opportunities that the older children had, such as going to college. Only she and the younger brothers did not have a chance to go to college.

Annette's grandparents died before she was born, but her Grandfather Terrell came from Holland and was said to have driven oxen and worn wooden shoes. Her grandmother came from France, and she came to America with her parents. She met and married Annette's grandfather, and they traveled in a covered wagon. Annette's mother was born in Bell County, Texas, near Houston, and they settled in Converse, Louisiana, sometime later. Her grandfather was John Raimond, and her grandmother was Annette Ferguson, a relative of the famous Ma Ferguson.

Miriam Amanda Wallace was born in 1875 and became the first woman governor of Texas. In 1899 at the age of twenty-four, she married James Edward Ferguson, also from Bell County, and she served as first lady of Texas during the gubernatorial terms of her husband (1915–1917), who was impeached during his second term in office. When her husband failed to get his name on the ballot in 1924, Miriam entered the race for governor of Texas. Her first and middle initials were M. A., which led to her supporters calling her "Ma" Ferguson. She assured Texans that if she was elected, they would get "two governors for the price of one," because she intended to follow her husband's advice. Ma Ferguson was inaugurated fifteen days after Wyoming's governor, Nellie Ross, so Ma became the second woman governor in the history of the United States.

Annette did not meet her mother's sisters or brothers except for the youngest brother named Arron Raimond, who lived in Arkansas and came to the farmhouse when she was very small. The family later heard that he had died in 1923.

Annette remembered that her dad had one brother named John Terrill and one sister named Irene Brock. Her father and his brother were both farmers and must have disagreed about so many things. Even the family name seemed to cause some trouble with bills and business, so much so that Annette's father changed the spelling of his name from Terrill to Terrell. It was still pronounced the same. Annette listed and discussed each of her brothers and sisters so Louie would know who she was talking about in her letters. They were Lilly, Clemon, Grover, Annie, Burchette, Lillian, Willie, Crowder, James, Melissa, John, Preston, and she was the last child.

CHAPTER 5

When his enlistment was completed, Louie turned toward the west to find his brother in California. He had written letters to his mother a time or two and found out that Everett was working at a steel mill in Fontana, California. Louie hitched rides for days in his uniform, which made it easier to get picked up until he reached the desert that he had to cross to reach California. He encountered a marvel of modern engineering on his trip when he found Plank Road. The first planks were laid in 1915, followed by months of workers hauling lumber to build two parallel tracks, each twenty-five inches wide, held together by wooden cross pieces spiked together to form a road. Traffic caused the plank road to take a beating over the next few months but proved that it could be done. In 1926 the highway commission built a new Plank Road with more funds, manpower, and equipment. The engineers abandoned the double-track plan and designed a roadway of wooden crossties laid to a width of eight feet with double-width turnouts every one thousand feet. The upkeep of the road proved difficult for the permanent maintenance force located at Gray's Well. Hard winds blew drifting sand across the road, and drivers were stubborn about sharing the highway. The road itself was bumpy and dangerous, but there was also a feeling of high adventure that was part of the new travel experience.

The traffic was so light on the wooden road that stretched across the barren wasteland that Louie had to walk for a long period of time. One day while he was walking on the wood planks that made up the roadway, a vegetable truck rumbled by on its way to deliver produce. With a little wave of his hand, he greeted the driver and continued walking until he happened upon a crate that contained iced lettuce. It was just his luck that Louie did not like to eat lettuce, so he scooped up some ice to cool his mouth and took a head of lettuce to occupy his time while walking. He pealed one leaf at a time until he reached the hard center of the head of lettuce and decide to take a bite. He ran as fast as he could back to the crate and grabbed as much lettuce as he could carry because it was so good.

Louie's brother was able to get a job for him at the steel mill, so he worked there for about two years before getting homesick and being overcome by the feeling that he wanted to head back toward Louisiana. He left his brother in California and began his journey back across the West. He came upon a bunch of people in the remote part of Arizona who drew his attention, so he stopped to see what they were doing. It happened that they were shooting a movie, and there was a little sign posted that read "Extras Wanted," which was something of interest to Louie, so he went about finding the person who could hire him. The role turned out to be in a cowboy movie. Louie and a few other extras were to hide behind a rock and shoot as the bad guys rode by on horses. In the next scene, he and the other men were to ride by the former hiding place on horses. So it happened that his film debut involved Louie shooting at himself in a cowboy movie.

He continued on his journey back to Louisiana with a trucker who said he would be going to Houston, Texas. That would fit into his plans very well because he had a brother named Aubrey who lived in Houston and worked in a hotel kitchen. He had a nice visit with Aubrey and Francis, his new bride, who also worked at the hotel, but Louie was ready to move on. Aubrey's wife was said to be a Bohunk, but Louie found her to be a lovely young lady and a gracious hostess during his visit.

Louie asked, "What is *Bohunk* suppose to mean?" and Audrey told him, "The word has been used to indicate that they are rough, stupid, or hunky, but is a slur for people of east central European descent. It is also used for Ukrainian immigrants during the early twentieth century," Audrey explained.

Louie told Audrey that he had a great gal and he was having a good visit, but he was ready to continue his trip. Louie thanked Francis for the much-appreciated kindness before heading to the nearest highway that pointed east. The first trucker to stop offered him a ride to Galveston, where he was to pick up a load at the docks near downtown. He was heading south, but he thought, *a little walk on the beach sounds good to me.*

CHAPTER 6

Louie Gray arrived in Galveston, Texas, before dark of a rather cool evening. It had been raining and he could see the public library from where the last ride dropped him off. He walked to the entrance and read a little sign stating that the library hours were from nine a.m. until nine p.m., which gave him four to five hours for a little research about the next leg of his journey. It was October 7, 1928, and Louie would be twenty-one years old in a few months. A large map on the wall indicated that there was a ferry boat to Bolivar Peninsula and a beach that ran along the Gulf of Mexico to a small town called Sabine Pass about forty miles away. The next town after that was Port Arthur, Texas, and Louie had a strong desire to go there. He stumbled onto some articles and stories about the history of Bolivar while looking for information about the area over which he must travel. There was an article about the Ice Age and how roving people lived in the area around 9000 BC. It was reported that broken pottery and arrow points were found that dated back to AD 1200 and relics of humans and extinct animals that covered an eleven-thousand-year time span. The writings of the French and Spanish as early as the 1500s recorded that Indians were found in the area.

In 1528 Alvar Nunez Cabeza de Vaca and his crew were exploring the Gulf of Mexico when a storm demolished the boats, and eighty to ninety men were washed ashore. They were naked, hungry, and exhausted by the ordeal and built fires to warm themselves. Some Karandawa Indians found them and brought fish and roots for them to eat and later took them to their cluster of huts. All but about fifteen of the Spaniards died of exposure and starvation that winter, which led to cannibalism among the crew. Half the Indians died of dysentery spread by the shipwrecked men, and the Karandwas would have killed the Spaniards except they believed that the men had some magical powers. De Vaca and his men were forced to act as healers and were enslaved for six years before he and a few of them escaped in 1534.

Louie's time in the library was running out, but he read that Jean Laffite had arrived in Galveston in 1817 and found the Karankawas were spending their summers at the west end of the island. He was sad to read that the Indians died in large numbers from tuberculosis, syphilis, measles, small pox, and other diseases spread by traders, explorers, and missionaries. By 1860 the last of the Karankawa ceased to exist.

As the library was closing, Louie made his way toward the waterfront of Galveston and found some beer joints that would be open most of the night. Slot machines were everywhere in the business establishments, so he tried his hand at the nickel machines.

When he started winning on the slots, it drew the attention of one of the girls who worked in a place called the Pirate's Cove Bar. She tried to strike up a conversation and insinuated that it could go a lot further, but Louie was tired from the long trip and needed to clean up and eat before he would feel like a human being again. With a handful of nickels, he parlayed his change into enough to have a meal, stay in a local hotel, and get breakfast the next morning. It was only a matter of city blocks to the ferry landing and an exciting ride across Galveston Bay to Bolivar. By the time the ferry reached the other side, Louie had found a new friend who offered him a ride as far as Crystal Beach. The new friend knew a lot about the ferryboats that served Galveston and some of their history, being a resident of the peninsula. He told Louie that the ferries across Galveston Bay, or Bolivar Roads, as it was called by the locals, started with Indians, pirates, and early settlers. A regular service was started when the railroad needed a way to move freight between the peninsula and Galveston. The ferries were just large barges that could accommodate a complete train. The Gulf & Interstate Railway completed a line in 1896 and used barges to cross Bolivar Roads carrying rail cars and passengers too. The barge that Louie boarded for the trip across Galveston Bay was named *W. E. Maxon,* and it was towed by a tug named the *J. W. Terry.*

He had gotten an early start that day and was lucky enough, or personable enough, to get to ride part of the way to Port Arthur where there might be a job in those hard times. He bid farewell to his new friend and started walking down the beach toward his destination. He happened upon some men building a couple of beach cabins and stopped to talk to them.

"We need some help with this construction," one of the men said.

"It will be all right with the boss if you want to earn some money for a fair day's work," said another man who seemed to be in charge of the crews.

Louie agreed that he would like to work with them to build the cabins, and he stowed his bedroll and clothes bag where they showed him. The workers had put up a shelter and made a little campsite because they would be there until the cabins were finished. Louie was introduced to oysters, clams, shrimp, and crabs that were fairly cheap on Bolivar. The workmen cooked crabs and shrimp in a big pot set up over the campfire each night, and the workers made a red sauce from Catsup, Tabasco, and Lea & Perrins. He enjoyed the shrimp and raw oyster dipped into the red sauce, along with the delicious boiled crabs. They would pitch in some of the money to buy potatoes and corn on the cob to go with the seafood when the vegetables were available.

The construction lasted another three months, and Louie earned enough money to travel in style, if he wanted. During the building, Mr. Leblanc, the owner of the cabins, visited the construction site and met Louie. He seemed impressed with the new man and offered him a job in his foundry in Port Arthur when the work at the beach was finished. Things were looking up for the wanderer. He even started thinking about the girl he had left in Shreveport, Louisiana, and decided that he would go back there and ask her to marry him as soon as he had a steady job. One of the men who were working on the cabins was from

Sabine Pass, which he said was a little town on the way to Port Arthur. He told Louie about a little seafood restaurant at the crossroads where he would turn left to head toward Port Arthur when he left Crystal Beach. He and Louie had time to talk of many things and discussed what they knew about the history of the area. Louie told him of the research he had done in Galveston, and his new friend Sammy told him what he knew about Sabine Pass and the area beyond.

"The town of Sabine Pass is thirty miles southeast of Beaumont, was first known as Sabine City, and was laid out as early as 1836. The Sabine City Company, which organized the town, included people such as Sam Houston and others that I cannot remember. The town was to be a major gulf seaport, and the first steam sawmill was established there in 1837. By the time of the Civil War, the town had a newspaper, the *Sabine Pass Times,* and a connection on the Eastern Texas Railroad to move cattle and cotton. The town was incorporated in 1861. Fort Sabine and Fort Griffin were constructed to fend off Union attacks, but a yellow fever outbreak in 1862 caused many residents to leave. There was a battle of Sabine Pass in 1863, a hurricane in 1886 that killed eighty-six people, and storms in 1900 and 1915 that limited the town's development and bright future. Arthur E. Stillwell tried to buy choice tracts of land from the Kountze brothers, but they would not sell," Sammy said with a sad note in his voice.

The cabin job was finally completed, and it was time for Louie to continue the trip to Shreveport with a little stop in Port Arthur to see about the job that was promised. He liked what he saw and took the job offer at Standard Brass but would only come back if

Annette was with him. When he arrived in Shreveport, he waited outside the telephone company where Annette worked. It had been a month or more since she had received a letter from Louie, and all she knew was that he was working on the beach and might get a job in Port Arthur. Soon he saw her walking with several girls as they left the building. Louie stood quietly until she realized that he was there. Annette ran to him and jumped right into his waiting arms.

She kissed him passionately, and all he said was, "Want to get married?"

CHAPTER 7

Annette and Louie were married on November 13, 1928, in Bossier City, Louisiana. For a wedding present, Annette gave him a gold Elgin pocket watch with a little Chinaman's face wearing a little cap that was the winding stem. Louie was proud of the watch and planned to pass it along to his son someday. Besides a one-carat wedding ring and a platinum wedding band, Louie bought Annette a dinner ring with a small single diamond in the middle of a diamond-shaped black onyx. They both had earned good money for those days and were able to start their lives on top of the world.

The newlywed couple moved to Port Arthur, Texas, and took an apartment not far from Louie's job with Standard Brass Company. The young couple had all they needed to start a family and earn a living.

In October 1929 the stock market crashed, wiping out 40 percent of the paper values of common stock, but politicians and leaders continued to make optimistic predictions for the nation's economy. Business houses closed their doors, factories shut down, and banks failed. By 1933, approximately one out of every four Americans was unemployed. Louie was working and had Annette quit her job to start a family with their first son, Louie Jr. Patricia and Gail were later added to their little family. Annette worked at the telephone company until Louie Jr. was born, and Louie worked all the hours he could at the foundry. He was fortunate enough to sell some of the products that his company made to help employees through the Depression. As part of his job at the Standard Brass, items such as cast-iron cooking pans, cornbread molds, and pots were made to enable the employees to earn money during a hard time. The presidential election of 1932 was chiefly a debate over the causes and remedies of the Great Depression. Hebert Hoover was unlucky enough to enter the White House only eight months before the stock market crashed. He struggled tirelessly but ineffectively to get the wheels of industry into motion again. His opponent, Franklin D. Roosevelt, was prepared to use bold experimental remedies for recovery and won the presidential election. Roosevelt took office in 1933 with an air of confidence and optimism with a program known as the New Deal. Millions of Americans were out of work by 1933 when Congress passed the Agricultural Adjustment Act (AAA) to provide economic relief to farmers. Work relief came in the form of the Civil Works Administration (CWA) and the Civilian Conservation Corps (CCC) to bring relief to young men between eighteen and twenty-five years old in the work camps around the country. So many disasters were happening around the country and the world, but in Port Arthur and in

Texas, oil helped to carry the state through an otherwise devastating time in history.

Louie Jr. was ten years old when the Gray family planned a day at the beach on a Saturday in 1939. Their firstborn, Louie Jr., was his dad's pride and joy, and Annette was the perfect housewife and mother for the little family. Patricia and Gail helped their mother prepare the fried chicken, potato salad, and watermelon, so it was ready to pack into the car for the trip to Bolivar Peninsula, which was the place Louie liked to go for a beach outing with the family. He repeated the story of how he was walking down the beach many years ago and had stopped to help some guys build beach cabins. He always told how that led to a job at the Standard Brass in Port Arthur. Then he and Annette would remember how Louie came to get her in Shreveport and they were married. Over the next years, the young couple developed friends and had visits from relatives from Shreveport, Houston, and Beaumont. Johnny Beard was a friend who would come and stay when he was in the area, and one of Annette's nephews called Dago lived in Beaumont and would visit on Sunday afternoons. They attended Central Baptist Church, which was close enough to their home to walk during the lean times.

It was a beautiful morning as they left Port Arthur on that August 31, so the day was going to be hot, a good time to romp in the surf and have the great meal that Annette had brought along. They passed a little fishing town called Sabine Pass on the coast and headed along the Bolivar Peninsula until it was time to turn off the highway onto the sand. They drove along slowly, looking for a good spot to make their little camp, and when Louie located it, he parked the car heading toward the Gulf of Mexico. As soon as they were out of the car, the kids wanted to run to the water. Annette spread an old blanket on the sand and unloaded the trunk of the car.

Jr. called to his dad, "Hurry up and get to the water so we can play in the waves," as he ran toward the surf. Louie did not take long to join him, and they started playing one of their favorite games of jumping into the waves from his dad's shoulders, and that is when it happened. Jr. jumped from Louie's shoulders, but instead of diving into the wave, the trough moved in under him and Jr. hit the shallow water between waves. His dad pulled him from the water and shouted to Annette, "Honey, come help me with Jr." It was already too late because Jr.'s neck was broken, and he was no longer breathing by the time his mother arrived.

Panic set in, and Louie ordered, "Honey, pack the car and get the girls so we can take Jr. to a hospital in Galveston." His mother held him all the way to the Bolivar ferryboat and to the emergency room of the hospital, but there was nothing that could be done to save him.

The return home was a bitter event. Louie did not want to leave his son in Galveston, but the doctors insisted that it must be handled properly. Jr. was buried in a cemetery in Port Arthur a week later, but Louie would never recover from the loss of his only son.

CHAPTER 8

After the death of Louie Jr., life had to go on. Louie stopped at Jones Smoke House on his way home from work, drank more beer than before, and smoked two packs of cigarettes a day. Annette had to go and get him more often because he was too drunk to drive home. He would never get over the loss of his only son, but on April 25, 1942, a little visitor came along that helped ease the pain. His name was James Travis Gray, and they decided to call him Jim.

Jim was the youngest child of Annette and Louie Gray and became the baby of the family. Louie was proud of the little cotton-topped boy and would take him into his work area to show him off every chance he got. The two older sisters thought of him as a doll to play with and had him in a dress until he was three years old. Mechanical things intrigued him, and Jim had a desire to see how everything worked. He would disassemble toys, bicycles, and the family car to see what made them function. He traced electrical circuits and symbols from engineering books and had to know the purpose of the components. It was no surprise that Jim wanted to go into engineering after high school, but something happened that affected the rest of his life.

His dad Louie was a hard-working, hard-living man. His job at the foundry in Port Arthur was hard and dirty, but he loved his family and wanted to provide the best he could. He and Annette had gone through the Depression period and World War II together, so by the 1950s, Louie was seeing his hard work pay off. They had a house in a good neighborhood, a new car, and three children who were popular with their peers. When Louie got home to the house on Eleventh Street, he liked to sit in his favorite chair by the front door of the house, smoke a Camel, and listen to the radio. Jim would climb into his dad's lap on those occasions and ask to see the gold watch. He was especially thrilled when Louie would open the back of the watch so Jim could see inside. He liked to see the jeweled works inside the watch and study the movement of the balance and gears. Years went by and Jim saw the watch from time to time and admired the little Chinaman's face whose hat was the winding stem under a loop at the top of the watch. When he was about ten years old, which would have been around 1952. Jim asked, "Dad, I have not seen your watch lately." "Can I see it?"

"I no longer have the watch." "I sold it to Sonny Metcalf when money was tight."

"Can you find out if it can buy it back?" "I have saved twenty silver dollars." A couple of nights later, Louie told Jim to jump into the car and they would go see Sonny Metcalf about the watch. When Mr. Metcalf came to the door, Jim asked, "How much would you take for the watch, Mr. Metcalf?"

"You can have it for free because the kids have damaged it." It had a broken face, the crystal was missing, the hands were missing, and the stem loop was gone. Jim could not wait until Saturday when his dad would take him to the jeweler's downtown to see about getting the watch fixed. The jeweler looked at the broken watch and said, "We can't fix it here, but it can be sent to the factory for repair." Several weeks went by before Jim received word that the watch was ready for pickup. He brought his life savings of twenty silver dollars with him to the store and asked the price of the repair. The store manager told him that it would be twenty dollars, so Jim counted out his money to reclaim a family heirloom.

Then Louie suffered his first heart attack and could not work. Jim had been working at Retting Ice Cream Parlor on Proctor Street since he was eleven years old. After school and on weekends, Jim would ride his bicycle to work the seven p.m. to eleven p.m. shift. While Louie was in the hospital, Jim would pack his favorite ice cream and ride to St. Mary's Hospital to deliver the treat to his dad's room. There was not much in Port Arthur that Jim could not get into, and by slipping in a side door and up the back stairs, Jim could be at his dad's room in twenty minutes. It was a time when Jim and his dad could talk without interruption and on a man-to-man basis. Jim learned how to be a man from his dad's words and actions.

Louie spent about six weeks in the hospital but was finally able to come home to recuperate, or that is what he was told. There was not much that could be done for a man with a failing heart in those days, so on

February 28, 1955, the fatal attack came while he was working on a stamp collection that he and little Jim had started together years before.

Patricia, the oldest daughter, was married and living out of state while the youngest daughter was about to get married. Soon Jim and his mother were left alone to make ends meet. Annette worked three jobs to pay off debts and provide the necessities while Jim worked nights and weekends at the ice-cream parlor and later at a hamburger stand while finishing high school.

CHAPTER 9

Louie Gray opened his eyes and found that he was still in bed on this Saturday morning in 1938. He had promised the family that they would have a day at the beach, and Louie needed to get away too. He had been working too hard and chose to stay at Jones Smoke House a little too long last night. He rolled out of bed and made it to the bathroom just in time, and as he walked back into the semi-dark bedroom where Annette was still sleeping, he saw a figure in front of him.

Startled, but not scared, he exclaimed, "What the hell are you doing in my house?"

The ghostly figure answered, "Do not be frightened, Louie. I am here to prevent a misfortunate accident that will happen today if you don't heed what I say." Louie remembered something similar happening to him before, and he had taken the advice of this mysterious figure so long ago.

"Tell me what is to happen and what can I do to prevent it," asked Louie.

The figure told him, "There will be a disaster if you let Louie Jr. jump from your shoulders into the surf today." "Play in the water with Jr., but do not let him jump from your shoulders because he will die."

When Jim thought that his dad fully understood, he faded away, leaving Louie standing in the early morning light filtering through the wooden blinds on the bedroom windows.

It was a beautiful morning as they left Port Arthur on that August 31, so the day was going to be hot. They entered a fishing town called Sabine Pass on the coast, and Louie decided to take a little detour to Dick Doweling Park, which was another one of their favorite things to do. The kids climbed on the statue of the civil war hero and watched the ships move into and out of the inter-coastal canal that was by the park. After a little time to enjoy the park, Annette suggested, "Let's go on down to the beach now." The small family proceeded along the Bolivar Peninsula until it was time to turn off of the highway onto the sand. They drove along slowly looking, for a good spot to make their little camp, and when Louie located it, he parked the car heading toward the Gulf of Mexico. As soon as they were out of the car, the kids wanted to run to the water. Annette spread an old blanket on the sand and unloaded the trunk of the car.

Jr. called to his dad, "Hurry up and get to the water so we can play in the waves," as he ran toward the surf. Louie did not take long to join him, and they started to play one of their favorite games of jumping into the waves from his dad's shoulders. But that is when

Louie remembered what the ghostly figure had told him about letting Jr. dive into the waves.

He told Louie Jr., "Instead of diving into the waves, let's just play in the rough surf today." It was not long before they were roughhousing in the water, and Louie threw Jr. into one of the waves, but he landed on his arm and broke it. His dad pulled him from the water and shouted for Annette, "Honey, come help with Jr." With the help of his wife, Louie set the bone right there on the sand and made a sling from a beach towel.

Louie ordered that the car be packed immediately and announced that they would take Jr. to a hospital in Galveston. His mother held him all the way to the Bolivar ferryboat and to the emergency room of the hospital, where the doctor told them that the bone was already set and he would just wrap the arm and put on a cast for the trip home.

The return home was much calmer than the trip across the ferry and to the hospital in Galveston. They stopped at a roadside table under a tree and had the lunch that Annette had fixed for the beach, and the whole event became another one of the family stories that started, "One time we were at the beach …"

CHAPTER 10

A few months after Jim's trip back to 1986, Missy, the family dog, developed health problems. She was fifteen years old by then and had developed a lump on her back that started to interfere with her walking. Jim knew that it was just a matter of time before they would lose old Missy. This black Labrador retriever loved the family and the grandchildren, plus she was the best dove-hunting dog Jim had ever seen. She would sit quietly with Jim until the birds started to fly on those early-morning hunts, and then she expected him to shoot down one or two. If he did not shoot when she thought he should, Missy would turn an inquisitive look toward Jim, as if to say, "Why didn't you shoot that one?" If Jim took a shot, she was halfway to the bird before it hit the ground. Missy and Jim went hunting every year for the fifteen years of her life, and now it was time for her to go.

Jim and the rest of the family did not want to see her die. The grandchildren called her Missy Puppy and could lay on her or hug her any time they wanted. Thinking of the early experiments, Jim wondered if Missy's spirit could be separated from her old aged body and come to live with them. It was worth a try.

The equipment used for the development of the larger chamber and system was stored in the back room at the lab and was scheduled for disposal. It was not much trouble to load it into the back of his pick-up and bring it to the farm. He was head of the research group by then, and no one would miss the old prototype equipment.

The prototype equipment was brought to the farm and placed inside one of the old outbuildings. The power requirement was not very high, so a 220-volt wire was run from the existing 200-amp breaker box to provide the electrical needs of the extraction process.

There was no need to have hospital or even laboratory cleanliness to perform the process because there was no danger of contamination. Missy had to be carried to the table and lay still as Jim placed the electrodes to her head and body. Separation of the spirit from Missy's sickly body did not take long, and the ghostlike figure began to appear in the small chamber that had been used in the early experiments. She seemed confused and trapped in the chamber until Jim signaled to her to come to him. For the last couple of years, Missy could not hear, and Jim directed her by signs that she understood. Now, she was free of the bodily constraints and jumped to the ground and came to Jim. He stooped down to pet her as he had done so many times over the years, but she was more like a vapor than substance. She danced around like a puppy and was so glad to be free of all pain and restraint of her old body. As Jim had counted on, she had no desire to fly away and leave the family that she loved and that loved her. How to explain a ghost dog living at the farm and whether her spirit could be placed in another body were worries for another time.

CHAPTER 11

Missy the ghost dog was her usual happy self, except it was hard for her to get used to not being petted or fed twice a day. She enjoyed following Jim everywhere he went or running ahead through the woods to the lake. She was well behaved in the boat while Jim fished, and she responded to family voices as if she had a material body. The grandkids came to the farm and learned to accept that she was still Missy but in a different form.

Jim became friends with a veterinarian named Bill Hopper in the little town where they lived, and they eventually got around to discussing Missy the ghost dog. Everyone around the little town called Bill Hopper "the Doc." Jim's new friend Bill could not believe it at first, but seeing was believing for the vet, as it turns out. Before long, the two men discussed the possibility of putting Missy into another dog's body just as if they were talking about a flea dip for one of Bill's patients.

Jim had the equipment to extract the spirit from a small animal but had no way to keep the subject alive until the spirit transfer could be made. Doc had all the equipment needed to keep a dog's body alive while a new spirit was inserted, and he seemed to be willing to help with the process.

The day came when Doc called and told Jim that he had a potential subject for the transfer of Missy's spirit. A small black dog would be available that had a lot of Labrador retriever in her, along with the possibility of a little bulldog. It had been ordered by a judge that the dog was to be destroyed because she bit someone within Tyler County. The task had been assigned to the Doc, and they had ten days to carry out the procedure.

Working in the Doc's offices would be more convenient and provide better cover for the euthanizing, connecting to life support, and the concealment of Jim's equipment. The office even had a crematory that would complete the plan to use the body of the bad dog for Missy's spirit.

The night of the big caper finally came, and Missy was happy as a lark to get into the car with Jim for the trip to the Doc's office. She apparently could not smell anymore in her ghost state because she usually stopped dead at the door of a vet's office. It took usually two people to get her into the waiting room because she hated the smell so much. The bad dog was already asleep when the Doc let Jim and Missy into the office and led them to the examining room. This time, Missy just followed Jim's lead and got into the chamber as Jim directed. When all was ready, the Doc closed off the bad dog's air passages, and it was soon clinically dead. The life support equipment was started, and Jim began to reverse the process that was used to extract Missy's spirit from her old diseased body only a few months ago. The ghostlike apparition disappeared from the chamber, and the two men held their breath while they waited for signs of life from the bad dog's body on the table. The black tail began to move then bang against the table in an effort to wag. Then her eyes opened, and the Doc gently removed the breathing apparatus from her muzzle. Seeing that she was breathing on her own, the electrodes and monitors were disconnected from the little dog's body, and she raised her head to look around the room. Jim began to pet her head, and she went into her "glad to see you" act that only Missy could perform.

CHAPTER 12

The friendship between the two men developed after Jim's retirement from the laboratory work, and soon the Doc was confiding in Jim about how he missed his wife of four years. She had died in a car wreck on Highway 190, just outside of Woodville one night on her way home from a visit to Houston. She was buried in Mt. Pisgah Cemetery off Seneca Road, and he had visited her gravesite almost every day for the last two years. To have a friend like Jim helped him in his time of loneliness, and the two talked about the science of spirit travel.

The idea to go back and save the Doc's wife seemed to evolve from the procedures performed on Missy and the confidential discussions of how Jim saved his son from being murdered after the fact. One obstacle to going back and saving the Doc's wife was access to the equipment necessary to make the trip, so the two men began to plan how to construct the apparatus needed for spirit separation.

With the Doc having a place to conceal the project and the money to finance the items needed, Jim's expertise would make it possible. There were patents on the process in Jim's name but were held by his former employers. Their idea was to use the technology for personnel secret work and not for commercial gain. Jim drew the plans for the components that had to be built, and the items could be called by other names to get them manufactured. One of the larger items was the chamber with dimensions of thirty-six inches in diameter by seventy-eight inches tall made of one-inch-thick acrylic material. Other costly items, such as the anode and cathode, had to be purchased and were to be made of pure platinum so that it could heat red-hot without melting. There was a seal at the top and bottom of the chamber tube and a base for the thirty-six-inch-diameter tube so that a partial vacuum could be maintained. The power requirements were available in the commercial center where the Doc's office was located, and so the plan moved forward with Operation Rescue, as they called it. The Doc ordered additional power into his examining room so they would have the necessary 500-amp, 460-volt, three-phase service installed by the time the components were finished.

While they worked, Jim asked the Doc what his wife, Mandy, looked like and how he could convince her to avoid the drive home on that fateful night. The Doc showed Jim photographs of Mandy and suggested that he meet her at the Kelsey-Seybold Clinic on Highway 6 in Houston where, she would be at three thirty p.m. on February 28. If she left the clinic alone and started the drive to Woodville, she would be killed by a truck that veered over the centerline on Highway 190 at approximately seven p.m. He described the white Toyota that she would be driving and the license plate with letters that spelled DOCMATE.

The Doc described Mandy in a sad voice, "She is very beautiful with long red hair and green eyes. She is average height and build, but heaven is in her arms for me." Then he related, "She was hurrying home to tell me that she was expecting our first child." "It was going to be a surprise for me when she got home."

"How can I tell Mandy what is to happen to her on the way home and prove to her that you have sent me to save her from the wreck?" Jim asked the Doc as they worked on the machine for what seemed like an eternity. The two of them rehearsed a little script to use when Jim met her, and they practiced and refined it as the days went by.

Jim decided to wait for her in the car so that no one would see him or hear him try to explain to Mandy.

He was hidden in the backseat of the car when Mandy slid into the front seat and fastened her seatbelt.

"Don't be afraid, and don't jump out, Mandy," Jim said. "I have been sent by your husband to tell you something important." "Do you understand, and will you listen to me?" After what seemed like a long time, she said, "I will listen to you, but who are you?"

Jim knew identifying himself would be the hard part; how would he make Mandy believe that the Doc had sent him?

"Mandy," Jim said, "you don't know me now, but we will meet some years from now in Woodville." "I am a friend of your husband, Bill Hopper, and he sent me to save your life." "Something really bad will happen if you drive up Highway 59 and turn onto Highway

190 later tonight." "You can call the Doc, but it will do no good now because he will not know about what is happening here until much later." "We have talked about how to tell you and what to say, but it was hard to predict your reactions, so I can only suggest that you drive to a friend's house and call the Doc and tell him that you are staying over tonight and will drive on in the morning." "He will ask why are you staying over and you can tell him that the car is acting up so you left it at a shop near your friend's house and was told that it will be ready in the morning." "If he wants to come to Houston and get you, there is no problem with that, but do not go back to Woodville tonight." It was like Mandy had been holding her breath since Jim first talked to her; her eyes were as big a saucers. Mandy was stunning. Along with her red hair, there was a hint of freckles on her nose. Jim could see why the Doc missed her so much and would spend all of his money to bring her back. When Mandy finally expelled a breath and drew in another one, she said, "This whole story is so far-fetched, but I want to hear more."

"How did Bill tell you to prove who you are?" she asked. "I know him, and he would have given me some sort of sign, word, or detail."

"You are right, Mandy." "He told me to tell you that on your wedding night, he had worked with so many animals in veterinarian school that he did not know how to make love except doggie style." Jim snickered.

She laughed and started to relax a little when she said, "No one knows that but me and Bill, so I will do as you suggested."

Time for the return trip was running out for Jim.

He did not know what would happen if he did not get back into his body in the allotted time, and he did not want to find out. He moved through time and space to the clinic in Woodville, but it was hard to remember where he was going and why. As his spirit entered the chamber and the ghost figure appeared, he thanked God that he had been allowed to travel on a trip of mercy, a trip that would make his newfound friend have a renewed life.

Jim barely remembered being inside the chamber for a few minutes before the Doc performed the procedure to bring him back to the world of the living. He woke gradually, and his first words were, "Did we bring Mandy back?"

The Doc said, "I have not had time to check for Mandy, but I do feel different and better than I have in years." "We did not talk about the way we will check to see if the mission of mercy was successful." "What if I call our house and see what happens?"

He dialed the phone and waited through two rings before Mandy's sweet voice said, "Hello, this is the Hopper residence."

The Doc was so excited that he could only say, "Honey, stay where you are and I will be right there." He was shaking so badly that Jim offered to drive the Doc home to see Mandy, and as they drove, the Doc said that he could see the things that had happened since Mandy was killed changing in his mind.

Even though Jim protested because he felt that the Doc needed to meet Mandy alone, the Doc insisted that Jim come in and meet her. When they were introduced, Mandy said she felt as though they had met before, but she was not sure when.

Mandy was back home safely, and the Doc was

ecstatic about it. About then, a young boy entered the room and said, "Hi, Dad. Want to go outside and throw the ball?" Memories started to flood into his head of a son he had never seen before. The Doc was remembering the birth and early childhood of his boy and thanked God that his family was safely with him. Jim bid farewell to the happy family and slipped out the door.

CHAPTER 13

Jim and Doc Hopper planned the trip back to 1924 so Jim could make sure that his dad received the telegraph from his mother and made the right choice to travel to Shreveport. The trip went fine, but Jim wondered if he could make more than one stop on a trip like that. Could he also stop in 1939 to warn his dad about Louie Jr.'s fatal accident? Jim was ready to test the theory of how much time a spirit could be absent from the body before it would have to join the spirit world, but to be safe, he spent a few minutes in 1924 and then a few minutes in 1939 to accomplish two missions with one trip. Some of the experiments with comatose people during his years with Medical Research Services and Medinautics seemed to indicate that any amount of time over two hours was getting into a dangerous zone for recovery. Jim stayed out of his body over two hours when he warned his son, Mitch, and stayed with him for the trip to Woodville that night in 1986. He not only lost the desire to return to the body but also had trouble remembering the details of where and when he was to return.

The trip to tell his dad that his son, Louie Jr., would die also went well and Jim returned to his body again in the offices of his partner. The traveling had accomplished the main objectives of Jim and the Doc so they decided to shut it all down for a while and suspend any more trips to the past.

Jim and the Doc had depleted their funds on the time travel project and equipment. Jim was retired on a pension from the Herman Memorial Foundation in Houston after it had taken over the company that he had worked for many years. The amount of his income was barely enough to live on, but it did not cost too much to live on the farm. The Doc still had his practice and would recover in time. Jim still wanted to develop more equipment and do more experimenting, but the money was not available for the foreseeable future. An employee of the veterinarian clinic named Karen Reyes had snooped around the equipment and overheard discussions about what was being done with the recent additions to the laboratory by Jim and the Doc.

Word gradually slipped out, and rumors started flying. One day out of the clear blue sky a man named Juan Reyes, Karen's uncle, came to Doc's office with a proposal. He had lost his only son in a wreck on Highway 190 when three young soldiers were driving from Fort Polk to Austin area on a training exercise. The Humvee military vehicle hit a tree when the driver tried to avoid a pick-up truck that had pulled out in front of him during a hard rain. Three white crosses mark the spot on Highway 190 between Woodville and Livingston where the Humvee flipped over and hit the tree that took the three young lives.

This distraught father said that he would give anything to get his son back and gave the Doc an idea how to help someone while getting more funds to continue the work. Doc told Mr. Reyes, "It might be possible to help you." He called out, "Karen, please come to my office," over the intercom. "First" explained the Doc, "all discussion and rumors about what is being done here must stop immediately if you want our help." "I will talk to Jim Gray, and meanwhile, I want you two to get the phone numbers of the other two families that lost their sons that night."

The Doc called Jim as soon as the little meeting was finished and said, "Jim, we need to meet as soon as possible." It did not take Jim long to finish the job he was doing at the farm and clean up for the trip to town. As soon as Jim walked in, Doc said, "I have an idea for helping three families at one time while asking for a reasonable fee. This will provide funds so we can continue the Time Shift projects."

"I think we should leave the fee up to the parents of the boys," suggested Jim, "but the laboratory must be moved to a secure location." Jim had come to realize that their present setup was too vulnerable, and he was becoming paranoid about who might show up one day to take over their experiments.

When Mr. Reyes reported the phone numbers of the other two families, the parents of the three boys who were killed on Highway 190 on June 19, 2006, were each called by Jim and the Doc in the following days. They were asked to attend a meeting in Woodville to discuss their sons and were assured that it was for their own good. It was not easy for these grieving parents to accept such an invitation, so Mr. Reyes was sent to Arkansas and Oklahoma to meet with the other two families and to assure them that the trip was necessary. He had met them during the ordeal of body identification and the release for burial, so his insistence to attend a meeting was more convincing than that of Jim or the Doc.

At the meeting in Woodville, the three families were told of the possibility that Jim could stop the tragic accidents from occurring.

"Folks, each of your boys will have to be convinced not to continue the drive that fateful night if this is to work. "Tell me about your financial situation. Tell us how much it would be worth to have your sons back and about your present ability to pay."

"I know that this sounds like an extortion scheme," Jim said, "so there will be no money paid until your sons are home safely." "Put the money in an envelope with Doc Hopper's address written on the outside and keep it with you until you see your son." "When this is over, you will be confused, so just remember to mail the money so our work can continue."

"Now," said Jim to Mr. and Mrs. Reyes, "tell me some things about your son and what would convince him to believe what I tell him."

Then Jim turned to Mr. and Mrs. Hockman, "What can you tell me about your son?" Finally, Mr. and Mrs. Barajas were questioned for details about their son.

Jim told the Doc, "It looks like we must use your office laboratory one more time, but if we can get the money, we will move the facility as soon as possible."

CHAPTER 14

By using the existing equipment still set up in the Doc's office, Jim prepared for the trip to 2006 to try and save the three young soldiers from being killed in the military vehicle wreck on Highway 190. The exact date and time were verified, and each parent signed a statement about paying the agreed amount when their boy returned alive. Also included in the statement were questions about what the boys would believe to be true when Jim talked to them. The form contained pertinent information about each boy and a photograph so Jim could be sure he was talking to the right guys. One of the parents furnished the description and identifying number of the Humvee that was being driven by one of the boys and a little-known fact that the boys stopped in Jasper at a Burger King around eight p.m. before continuing their drive westward.

Jim and the Doc checked all the Time Shift equipment one last time, and then the Doc prepared Jim for the trip through time and space. Jim had decided that being at the Burger King just before eight p.m. and getting into the vehicle with the boys when they stopped would be the best chance to talk to them.

Jim watched as they drove into the burger place and got into the rear of the Humvee as soon as it stopped rolling.

“Men,” said Jim, “don’t get out.” “Listen to me; that’s an order.”

The boys were so surprised that they sat still like they were at attention while Jim continued his monologue.

“I am here to save your lives and will prove it by telling you each something that your parents told me to use as proof.” “You, PFC Hockman, have a scar on your arm that is the result of a bicycle crash when you were eight years old,” said Jim to the first one. “You, PFC Reyes, almost drowned when you were about ten years old and your dad had to pull you out of the pond and do mouth-to mouth- resuscitation or you would be dead.” “PFC Barajas, you told your mom a secret before you left home, and I will repeat it, if you need me to relate it now,” Jim said, looking for his reaction. PFC Barajas told Jim, “I believe you.” “Why you are here and what do you want?”

Jim had been trying to come up with a way to avoid the accident between Woodville and Livingston. It had to be something that would delay their trip until the next day at least. What would be better than a wreck that killed the boys than a wreck that would save the boys? He told them about the fatal wreck they would have and the location so that they could understand that a planned, controlled wreck could save their lives and provide the delay needed to keep them away from what was to happen about an hour from now.

“You will be crossing a bridge over water between

here and Woodville where you can run the vehicle into the lake," Jim explained, "or you can find a place to run off the road anywhere that seems good to you." "You must disable this vehicle and not continue your trip tonight." "Will you do it to save your lives?" Jim asked. The leader of the three boys agreed, "This situation cannot be ignored, so we will stage a wreck after we leave Jasper heading toward Woodville, Sir."

Leaving the three boys to obey his command, Jim returned to the chamber and the Doc greeted him as his mind cleared from the Time Shift experience. It usually left him in a daze for about two hours, and shortly after that amount of time, Jim asked the Doc to call each of the parents and ask about the boys.

With the signed forms in hand and while the memory of losing their sons was still strong in their minds, each family mailed the money to the Doc's office, so the work to move the facility could become a reality. The three boys had no memory of being killed on Highway 190 but knew that the ghostly figure had saved their lives when their parents related the story of their deaths and burials. Each one called Doc Hopper on the phone and said thank you for their chance to see the future. PFC Reyes said he had plans to go to college after his military hitch and marry his childhood sweetheart after he got an education. PFC Barajas was being promoted to corporal and was getting ready to go to Iraq for a tour of duty. PFC Hockman was getting married and planned to make a career of the military.

The next time Jim drove toward Livingston, he looked for the three little white crosses that had been there for years. He was so happy that the crosses and the flower arrangements left by loved ones were not to be seen anymore.

CHAPTER 15

Before the equipment could be moved from the Doc's office to the new location, a great amount of work needed to be done. Jim thought that an underground facility on the farm property would be the best way to go, and the Doc agreed. Some of the heavy work could be contracted out, and some could be done by Jim and Bill.

First, Jim analyzed the load on an underground structure and sketched the layout needed for the equipment and laboratory. The project had to be kept a secret, so there had to be ways to keep any contractor from spreading gossip about their project or purpose. Jim suggested that they purchase three metal containers like the ones used for ocean shipping. They were strong enough to be buried and offered a watertight structure to protect the equipment and personnel. The three containers arrived and were set in the south pasture. Jim and the Doc rented a backhoe and brought it to the farm on a trailer so no one would be involved in digging the large hole needed to install the containers underground. Following the plans that Jim made, they dug a trench into the barn and built a stairway for access to the containers that had been set side-by-side in the excavation. They built a tunnel in the open trench using heavy timbers and a top with corrugated metal. The air-handing system consisted of ductwork along the walkway and into the containers along with electrical power for lights and the Time Shift equipment. Concrete was poured on the corrugated metal to form a roof for the walkway and the space across one end of the containers. The dirt was pushed back over the hole and trench so the area could be graded to resemble the original pasture. Grass would soon grow over the dirt to finish the underground facility, and the barn would hide the electrical switchgear and air handling system. Within three months of hard work, the facility was ready for the equipment to be moved into it. One container was set up as an office space and break room, one container was set up with the equipment used for the Missy experiment, and the third container housed the human-size chamber equipment. Both Becky and Mandy helped with cleanup to make the new hidden facility into a livable compound. Their ideas, such as a small kitchen and rest area, were incorporated, as were suggestions to make the place into a laboratory instead of a hole in the ground, but it was not long before the reason for the move came to fruition.

Two government agents from NSA, who Jim called *No Such Agency,* appeared at the Doc's office with questions about experimental work that had been done at the veterinarian office. The Doc denied knowing anything about unusual happenings at his office and told them that they were welcome to inspect the premises. While the agents were looking around, one of them asked about the empty area that seemed to have been used for something, but of course, the Doc told them that it was being set up for laboratory expansion needed for his veterinarian practice. After the agents left, the Doc conducted business as usual but made a call to Jim and said that he and Mandy would be over around seven that night for their usual game of dominos. Jim knew that they did not have a usual game of dominos and accepted his call as a coded message that something was wrong and they could not discuss it by phone.

The Doc and Mandy arrived at the Gray farm near seven p.m. by way of some back roads just in case they were being followed. With the twists and turns of the dirt roads, they were sure that no one followed them into the long driveway to the farm. The four conspirators gathered around the dinner table as if to play dominos, and the Doc told them about the visit from the NSA agents. Becky suggested, "Time Shift activities should be suspended immediately to see if the NSA will lose interest." Jim and the Doc agreed, and Jim said, "Let's stop any travel for a while and plan our next moves carefully.

"I think we should make the underground facility harder to find by disguising the entrance and the air-handling system in case this place is searched."

"What about security cameras and more fencing?" Doc asked.

"Yes, let's button up the farm so we will know when someone is snooping around," Jim said.

"Let's not discuss the project or work being done

over the phone or at any other place except a secure location," Doc said.

Mitch Gray visited the farm on weekends when he was not traveling. Tess's girls, who were adopted by Mitch, were grown and gone while the boys, Michael and Stephen, were reaching their teen years. They also liked to come to the farm, but some weekends, there were activities that the boys did not want to miss. On this occasion, Mitch drove in from Houston by himself to help his dad and the Doc, who were working on a project at the farm. The Time Shift equipment was already concealed, and the work mainly consisted of setting up the office and hiding the entry to the facility. Jim decided to tell Mitch about the use of the equipment and answer his questions. Tess seemed to know a little about the mystery because she had some residual memory of Mitch being killed. Billy Edwards was Mitch's best friend until he was killed by his father-in-law in 1986, so when he heard that travel through time and space was possible, he said, "Dad, let me go back and save Billy."

Jim tried to evaluate the problems and ramifications that saving Billy might bring and told Mitch, "We will have to make it clear to Billy what he has to do if he wants to live." "The plan must be rehearsed and that there is usually a long training period before making the trip." "The dangers of not being able to make it back to the chamber are always present." Then Jim told his son, "Your mother and I lost you once, and we cannot go through that again. What if I go back and try to save Billy?"

Mitch thought about it and said, "I understand the risk, and maybe it is too much to ask that Tess and the boys go on without me, Dad." "I will tell you some things that Billy and I shared so you can convince him to do what you ask."

Jim asked him, "Where will Billy be a few days before that grievous date that Mr. Long shot him so I can prepare him early?"

Jim had a plan to save Billy and would have to make two stops to set up the scenario. "Let's finish what we are doing here today and I will plan to leave in the morning," he told Mitch and the Doc.

Early the next morning, Jim was prepared for the trip, and he had his plan set in his mind. The first stop would be to see Don Downs, his old buddy from high school. Then he would meet Billy Edwards at his mother's house where he and his wife, Lori, lived, according to Mitch.

The Doc arrived early the next morning to get Jim ready for another trip, and Mitch was assigned to do some of the routine procedures. The ghostly traveler first arrived at Don's house early in the morning to be sure he would be in his home office. That would be the best chance to see him, even if he planned to leave the home office to call on customers. Jim appeared inside the office and was glad to see Don busily going through invoices on his desk.

Jim said, "Don, don't be afraid because I am here as a friend to ask a favor."

Don asked, "Is that you, Jim?"

"Yes, it is me, and the favor involves a young man named Billy Edwards. He will be killed on Friday night if you don't help." Jim continued to tell him the whole story. When Jim finished explaining the situation and what he could do to stop the murder, Don said, "I owe you some favors, old buddy, so I will do what you ask."

Jim made the second stop a few minutes after leaving Don. This time it was inside the house of Bonnie Edwards, where Billy was expected to be at that time of morning. As luck would have it, Billy lay sleeping beside his young bride but awoke as Jim began to talk to him in a soft voice.

"Billy," Jim said to him, "Mitch sent me to help you through a bad situation that will happen this Friday night."

At first, Billy was speechless, and when he did regain his voice, he said, "I recognize you, Mr. Gray." "What is to happen, and what should I do to stop the bad thing?" Jim was surprised that he did not have to convince Billy of who he was or to do as he was told. Jim continued to tell him all about what would happen in a few days. Time was running short, but Billy seemed to understand what to do and seemed willing to do what must be done. Lori was still sleeping when Jim faded away.

The evening of February 28, 1986, found Billy, Lori, and Margaret heading to Mitch's apartment with some fried chicken. When Billy parked, he almost bumped into his brother-in-law, Earl Jr. A heated discussion ensued, and when Billy found out that Mitch was not in his apartment, the little group drove out of the Smiling Woods apartment complex in Billy's blue Mustang. He turned on Breen Road and headed toward Fairbanks North Houston Road when he saw a black Mazda turn the corner behind him. As he accelerated, gunshots rang out from the Mazda, and Lori realized it was her dad in the chase car. The Mustang pulled ahead of the Mazda, which gave them time to turn onto Fairbanks North Houston and into a little strip shopping center where they planned to call the police. The black Mazda and two other vehicles jammed in behind the Mustang, and Lori recognized her stepmother and her brother in the two other cars. As Billy stepped out on the driver's side of the car, Earl Long Sr. confronted him and began to rail him with cuss words and threats. Billy slipped a small revolver from his pocket and shot Mr. Long in the face. The bullet entered Long's cheek and took out part of his brain; he fell dead against the car and never uttered another word. When her dad had appeared at the driver's door of the Mustang, Lori had exited the right side of the car and run into the store to call the police. Billy pointed the gun at Lori's step mother and her brother with these words, "Don't move." "Don't reach for your guns." "We will wait for the police to arrive."

It did not take long for the first police car to enter the drive, and as soon as it did, Billy laid the gun on the pavement and raised his hands in the air. The police accessed the situation and saw the three cars blocking the Mustang. They found that Lori's brother and step mother both had guns and quickly took them into custody. Billy told the police, "Look in Mr. Long's belt for a handgun, and search the Mazda for additional weapons." They found a fully automatic assault rifle with boxes of ammunition and more handguns. Billy told the police that he shot in self-defense and would give a full statement at the station.

When Jim visited his friend Don, he asked if he still had the Charter Arms .38 caliber snub-nose pistol. He asked him to please make arrangements to give it to a young man named Billy Edwards when he called on the phone. Jim told Billy to call Don Downs at his phone number and ask for a loaded Charter

Arms revolver. He was also told that in order to live through this Friday night, he would have to shoot Mr. Earl Long Sr., and Jim suggested shooting him one time in the head. He explained what to do afterward killing Mr. Long and made suggestions about how to behave and what to say.

The storeowner saw what had happened, and Lori made a statement about her dad's rage that caused her to leave home. Lori's friend Margaret also corroborated the eyewitness account of the storeowner and supported Billy's statement that he shot Mr. Long in self-defense. The grand jury later reviewed the case and found that the evidence did not warrant a murder trial. All the guns on the scene were confiscated by the police, and Lori's brother and her stepmom were fined for carrying the firearms because there was not enough evidence that they had intended to shoot Billy.

When Jim reappeared in the underground laboratory, he explained all that he had done and how the plan had saved Billy's life. He said, "If Don and Billy do exactly what I instructed, it will prevent the wrongful murder." Jim suggested to Mitch, "Why don't you call Billy to see how he is doing?"

CHAPTER 16

The closed-circuit movie cameras were installed and the entrances into the farm property were fitted with remotely operated hardware for the gates that required an entry password or could be opened from the farmhouse. Becky watched the monitors while she did things around the house, and Jim could keep an eye on any intruders that might approach the farm when he was in the house or barn. A big black SUV approached the gate one morning and used the intercom to alert the house of their presence. Jim asked, "What is your business here?" "I am Special Agent Jeff Jones." "We would like to enter the property," the agent replied. Jim said, "Please wait where you are and I will come out to visit with you." As Jim walked up to the gate, the three men in the SUV stepped out and approached the closed gate as Jim asked, "What can I do for you?" One of the agents asked, "Mr. Gray, do you know Dr. Bill Hopper, the veterinarian in town?" Jim said, "Yes, I know the Doc." Another one of the

NSA agents asked, "Mr. Gray, do you know about any strange experiments Bill Hopper is doing at his office?" Jim answered, "No, I don't know of anything strange about my friend." After more of the questioning, Jim finally said, "Tell me what you are really looking for, and I will tell you if I know something about it."

The lead agent realized that the discussion was getting them nowhere, so he told Jim that three military men had been debriefed about a vehicle accident, and the Doc's name had been mentioned in connection with saving their lives in some bazaar way. In their investigations, Jim's name had come up, and with a little checking, they had discovered that he had been involved in medical research experiments. Being that Jim and the Doc were friends, they wanted to talk to Jim about his involvement. When they asked to come in and have a look around, Jim said, "Sorry, guys, but I don't let strangers come onto my place." Agent Jones handed Jim a business card and told him to call if he had any more information, and the agents left in their SUV. Jim knew that this was not the last of it.

Jim walked back to the house and told Becky about the agents and their investigation then called the Doc. "Hey, buddy," Jim started, "we need to talk about what we are going to do about the situation." "Can you and Mandy come now?"

When the Hoppers arrived at the farm, the four friends sat on the front porch and discussed the investigation by the NSA agency while Bill Jr. played with Missy in the yard. Several suggestions were considered. Mandy said, "Let's go into hiding and make sure that the Time Shift equipment is destroyed before the NSA can find it." Then Jim hit upon an idea that he thought might defuse the situation. "Let's call the agent that I met today and set up a meeting," Jim suggested. "What would we tell him, Jim?" the Doc asked. "The idea would be to misdirect the agency by telling them about the research at the companies that I worked for and introduce them to the key people in the research," Jim explained. "By getting them involved with the medical research groups, the heat will be directed to them" "Let's suspend all our Time Shift work for now and hide the equipment against any possible search of the farm." Jim reached for the phone to call Special Agent Jeff Jones.

CHAPTER 17

Jim did not want to involve Bill and Mandy more than necessary with the NSA investigation, so he made an appointment at Special Agent Jones' office in Houston for the following morning. As he made the two-hour trip to the NSA office, he rehearsed what he would say and what he would suggest for their next step in the investigation. He remembered the secrecy agreements he had signed over the years and would bring that into the discussion with the agents. He would suggest that the agents call on certain people in the research organizations to see what they could tell the NSA about their work, but Jim decided to say that he would not break his pledge to keep the research confidential. He gave them a few names and asked, "Can I introduce you to any of them?" Then he said, "Let me know if I can be of further help with your investigation." As he prepared to leave their offices, one more question or two were asked, but Jim said, "That is all that I know, but you can call me after you have talked to these people."

Just as he suspected, the research scientist and their supervisors in each of the companies told them that they worked on numerous projects, but Jim Gray was the expert in several of their studies. The NSA subpoenaed the records of two of the research companies and studied the work and findings for information that they could use. There was no record of Jim traveling in time and space, but the research clearly showed that was where they were heading. As he knew would happen, Jim was called in again and asked by agent Jones, "Would you be interest in working with the agency to use the technology that was acquired by NSA?"

Jim explained, "I am retired and do not plan on immersing myself in the work as I did some years ago. I would agree to act as a consultant and oversee the work until others are trained to take over." He demanded, "I must review everything that is done, and records must be kept that I can monitor. If the technology that has been developed is used for unethical purposes, I am out of here."

Eventually, an agreement was made to pay Jim a generous fee, and he asked that certain of the people he had worked with before be invited to join the team. Those certain people were the RX-7 group that had helped Jim make the first trip that became known as Time Shift. NSA provided people who were to be trained to travel in time and space to benefit the United States' interests, and at first it sounded all right. Jim was told that the plan was to save a man from being assassinated, so Jim helped to train the traveler to mentally handle what was about to happen and how to focus on returning to the chamber within two hours. The target date for the agent was

April 4, 1968 and the place was Memphis, Tennessee. Jim thought that it was a good thing that the NSA planned to help the civil rights movement and save Martin Luther King Jr. from being killed. Jim had access to the top-secret files because of his government clearance and the agreement with NSA that he be informed about each trip. Jim pulled the file one morning before others had arrived for the continued mission training that would soon take place. He opened it and began to read.

_____MLK FILE–TOP SECRET _____

Name: Michael King aka Martin Luther King, Jr.

Place of Birth: Atlanta, Georgia, United States

Date of Birth: January 15, 1929

Movement: African-American Civil Rights

Major Organizations: Southern Christian Leadership Conference (SCLC)

Notes:

1957–FBI began tracking King and SCLC; mutually antagonistic relationship with FBI personnel and especially director J. Edgar Hoover

1962–King's most trusted advisers were New York lawyer Stanley Levison who is involved with the Communist Party. Another of King's lieutenant, Hunter Pitts O'Dell has been linked to the Communist Party by sworn testimony before the House of Un-American Activities Committee (HUAC). Wiretaps placed on Levison's and King's home and office phones.

1963–FBI received authorizations to proceed with wiretapping from Attorney General Robert F. Kennedy. Hoover stated that, "King is the most dangerous and effective Negro leader in the country and that he is the most notorious liar in the country."

1964–Ralph Abernathy, a close associate of King's stated that he had a "weakness of women" and history professor David Garrow presented arguments supporting King's sexual affairs. FBI sent warnings to King anonymously to let him know that his conduct could become public, but he accepted the Nobel Peace Prize anyway.

Jim scanned through the next forty-five pages of documents and got the picture that Martin Luther King Jr. was a problem to the United States government in many ways. Then Jim saw a commentary by Alan Stang dated January 19, 2009 that became quite graphic and notes referred to his first book entitled *It's Very Simple: The True Story of Civil Rights.* Jim continued his reading and found that Mr. Stang had outlined five important aspects of King's career:

his Communist Party activities

the violence that always erupted in a King demonstration

his plagiarism

his sexual pathology

his pagan beliefs

King's sodomite secretary, who spent his entire life in Communist Party activities and who demanded that "more bloody Negro suffering should be encouraged so that squeamish northern Negroes would be horrified into line." Carl and Anne Braden, who also ran King's organization, were both convicted in Louisville of blowing up a house inhabited by blacks and blamed it on whites. James Dombrowski was another Communist who was also another white and who stayed in King's home. As Jim read, it became clear that there were many ties to the Communist Party and the KGB, so he concluded that these activities were of interest to the FBI and the NSA because they were detrimental to the interests of the United States.

Around eight a.m. the scientific team and the NSA agents started shuffling into the laboratory including Agent Jones. Jim asked him to step into his office for a discussion about the purpose of the mission and how it was to be accomplished. Agent Jones explained that it had been decided to have the traveler approach Police Chief Lackey and convince him to arrest King at the Lorraine Motel, room 306 no later than five p.m. and charge him with soliciting a prostitute by breaking in and photographing him in action. The traveler was to instruct the chief to have King taken to jail and held for twenty-four hours. James Earl Ray could also be arrested about three p.m. hiding with his rifle in some bushes near a designated building in sight of the balcony in front of room 306. After Agent Jones told Jim the plan to save King, he felt much better and directed the team to prepare for the mission that would be taking place the next morning. Agent Jones worked with Agent Bates, who be making the trip into the past, for the rest of the day and into the night to be sure he was ready for any contingency.

The next morning found everyone in their place and ready for the mission. It all went off without a problem, and the traveler returned in one hour and fifty-eight minutes with news that the mission had been a success. It was soon verified that King did not die that day in 1968 and the small group knew that there would be no Martin Luther King Day, which was a holiday set aside to honor the martyred hero, and it would give the NSA time to develop the evidence necessary to discredit King. Jim still did not feel right about the whole mission and again pulled the file marked MLK. He read the new information that the file now contained which discussed the true motives of the mission to save MLK.

The report covered King's plagiarism of the work of Jack Boozer, a fellow Boston University theology student that led to King being stripped of his degree. It was proven that King was a fictional character who was manufactured and maintained by the Communists who chose him, groomed him, used him, and protected him until he became too much of a liability. The shooter, James Earl Ray, was trained by the KGB to assassinate King before he became too much of an embarrassment. His putrid activities leaked out to the public such as when he was in Norway to accept the Nobel Prize, he was seen naked chasing a woman down the hallway of his Oslo hotel. Congressman William Dickinson said in the Atlanta Journal dated March 31, 1965, that King participated in "all-night sessions of debauchery" in church. On the night before he was to be killed, King hired prostitutes and paid for them with church money. King wrote about the divinity of Jesus Christ, the virgin birth, and the resurrection as being made up by the apostles because they loved him so much. King was not a real Christian and should have been in jail as a sexual predator. The NSA wanted him alive to face the charges being brought against him based on wiretaps and bugs by FBI Director J. Edgar Hoover. During the trial, Mrs. King requested that the personal evidence be sequestered until the year 2027 and the judge agreed. There were over sixty thousand censored pages that were later released and the rest were labeled obscene.

As Jim closed the file after reading only part of the updates, he realized that the NSA and the FBI had succeeded in exposing Martin Luther King and his real motives.

CHAPTER 18

Jim pulled two more files that caught his eye the next morning. One was marked JFK, which he took to mean Jack Kennedy, and the other was marked RK, which he took to mean Bobby Kennedy. There was the standard identification information on the first page of each file, and as he read some of the entries, he decided to close the files and put them back in the secured cabinet when he noticed a file labeled Obama. Jim pulled that file and began to read the recent entries:

According to an article by Lou Dobbs, Obama had signed a presidential determination allowing hundreds of thousands of Palestinians to resettle in the United States. Sure, what can go wrong when we allow hundreds of thousands of people who have been, as Mark Steyn memorably described, "marinated" in a "sick death cult" who voted for Hamas, and 55 percent of whom support suicide bombings live here and at the American taxpayer's expense. By executive order, on January 27, (federal register on February 4) Obama ordered the expenditure of $20.3 million in urgent migration assistance to the Palestinian refugees and conflict victims in Gaza to resettle in the United States.

Few on Capitol Hill took note that the order provides a free ticket complete with housing and food allowances to individuals who have displayed their overwhelming support of the Islamic Resistance Movement (Hamas) in the parliamentary election of January 2006 at US taxpayers expense. A review of Obama's most recent actions since he was inaugurated a little more than two weeks ago:

His first call to any head of state as president was to Mahmoud Abbas, leader of Fatah party in the Palestinian territory.

His first one-on-one interview with any news organization was with Al Arabia television.

He ordered Guantanamo Bay interrogation centers closed and all military trials of detainees halted.

He ordered all overseas CIA interrogation centers closed.

He withdrew all charges against the masterminds behind the USS Cole and 9/11.

Today we learn that he is allowing hundreds of thousands of Palestinian refugees to move to and live in the US at American taxpayer's expense.

Jim closed the file and replaced it without reading the whole thing. He hoped that the NSA could do something to save the people of the United States from extinction.

When Agent Jones arrived at the laboratory around eight a.m., Jim again asked him to come into his office. Jim told him, "I have decided to leave the

RX-7 project in your hands to resume my retirement at the farm." Jim was really just a well-paid employee and knew that he could not change the minds of NSA and their plans to alter history to suit their purposes. Not knowing how to explain his doubts about what they were doing, he felt that getting out from under the control of NSA was the only thing to do. Agent Jones said that he understood and wanted to keep Jim on retainer in case he was needed later.

On his way home to the farm, it came to him as he drove, "I think it would be useful to see where all this leads," as he started calculating the time and place he would like to visit using the equipment that was still hidden underground. He stopped by Bill Hopper's veterinarian office and told him that the pressure was off of them now and that he had resigned from the NSA team in Houston. He also asked the Doc if he would help him make another trip, and the Doc asked, "Where to now?"

Jim had been thinking about when and where he would like to go now. He started with the present year of 2009 and the election of a liberal democrat as president of the United States. Assuming that this administration would run its course and that it would be twenty years before the truth would be known; Jim decided that he would like to see the farm in Woodville in the year 2029. Jim and the Doc planned to meet on Sunday afternoon to reopen access to the equipment and discuss the plans.

The Doc, Mandy, and little Bill Jr., who was six years old now, arrived at the farm for lunch with Jim and Becky. The family did not need to know that they were planning another trip, so the Doc and Jim slipped out to the barn while Bill Jr. took a walk with

Missy down to the lake and the ladies were sitting on the porch talking. The entrance was well hidden and the ventilation ductwork was out of sight behind a false wall in the barn, but they were soon into the underground walkway to the three container box rooms. They sat in the subterranean office and discussed cleaning and testing the equipment before the trip and the things that Jim wanted to know about the next twenty years. The records of how the system operated, the trips that were taken and a training manual for anyone that wished to travel was also stored safely in the office. Jim had stored guns and ammunition in the office with enough supplies to hide there for a few days just in case the unexpected happened.

They decided on an early Friday morning for the trip to the future. Jim prepared himself mentally and had checked every detail of the equipment operation. Doc was able to do his part of extracting the spirit and guiding it back into Jim's body upon re-appearance in the chamber. If all went well, Jim would return in a couple of hours and report all that he had seen and heard. The ghost-like Jim appeared behind the barn that was now almost thirty years old so he could reconnoiter the yard and house to see who was there. He found a young man working on an electronic gadget in the shop area and approached him cautiously. Jim said, "Don't be afraid. I am just here to talk to you."

The young man looked up with some surprise and asked, "Who are you?" Jim answered with his name and statement about his mission and asked the boy's name. He said, "Mr. Gray, you would not recognize me now, but I am Bill Hopper Jr., and I know a little about your trips through time." He told Jim, "I was twelve years old when the government attacked the farm and killed you and my dad." Jim had to overcome the shock of that news, but asked to be filled-in completely about what had happened since the year 2009.

Bill Jr. outlined the major events that led to the present situation, "The record shows that liberals, blacks, and people with socialist ideas were so strong in the election of 2008 that they elected a president that promised to share the wealth by taking from the rich and distributing to the poor. He was sympathetic to Muslims and said he had Muslim relatives who deserved to practice their faith. They would pass gun control laws to stop the violent criminals, there would be a national health care system established to take care of everyone and the depression stricken industries would receive large sums of bail-out money. New Orleans with its black mayor and governor received $450 billion to rebuild after hurricane Rita and the automobile industry received so many billions of dollars, that I can't remember the total. The country went into deep depression that was caused by the liberals but was blamed on the conservatives. States were in debt and companies could not collect what the government owed them, yet the spending went on. The government used $700 billion of the people's money to buy failing banks after they had already botched their attempts to control the housing market lending institutes. More gun control laws were enacted, ammunition was cut off from the citizens, and everyone with any guns had to register them and use only registered ammunition. There were large company layoffs and many people lost their jobs ... unemployment was rampant. The Muslim population grew over the years under the president elected in 2008 until it was large enough to demand more rights while taking away the foundation of the United States. About eight years ago, the Muslims began killing the Infidels in the larger cities. When his plans were all in place, the president declared marshal law because of the anarchy that was brewing in the country. Armed soldiers went door to door confiscating registered weapons and searching many houses of people who were suspected of hiding their guns. If anyone resisted, they were shot or arrested without trial or rights. Being out in the country, we are still able to hide and survive for now."

Jim asked, "Where were the conservatives and the opposing political party during all of these atrocities?" Bill Jr. answered with a bit of history that Jim knew nothing about. He said, "During the presidential convention of 2016, there was a terrorist attack on the meeting place in Chicago, Illinois. Almost all of the conservatives were killed and those that survived were convinced that their lives were in danger if they opposed the liberal group. By this time, the second amendment was repealed and that evidentially placed you and Dad on the list to relinquish your guns. The military showed up here at the farm and began a search of the house and buildings. You resisted and fought for your rights with two nine-millimeter, semi-automatic pistols that dad said you always kept handy. It was reported in the news that you had helped the former NSA organization work against the liberal humanitarian government that was just trying to help the people of the United States. Dad called Mom with a message to run and hide with me and Mrs. Gray, who was visiting us in town that day. They escaped and are alive and well, but Dad was arrested and died while they said he was trying to escape some time later. The farm stayed vacant for over a year while the ladies and I lived together. When the banks failed, the government bought them and began to reveal their financial plan for the country. The liberal government and agencies introduced a one world currency and decided that an electronic implant would be necessary for anyone who wanted to do business in the global market."

Jim knew that his time was almost gone, and he had to prepare for his return to 2009. He told Bill Jr. about the underground Time Shift equipment and how to access the hidden entrance. He told him to read all of the notes and instructions that were in the office. "I wish there was more time to explain everything, but I always try not to exceed the two hour limit for each trip," Jim explained. Jim asked about his son Mitch and what had happened to him. He was relieved to hear that Mitch and Tess were living in a motor home so they could travel to companies wanting artwork, but he did not have anymore detail. Jim asked, "How do you survive and what do you do for a living." Bill Jr. replied, "Mrs. Gray suggested that my wife and I move out here to the farm and plant food that could be traded for other goods needed to survive." "Mom and Mrs. Gray come out here on a regular basis to help with the farming and to take the produce, chickens, and eggs back to town for sale and trade." With that little bit of knowledge, Jim told Bill Jr. that he must go because his time had run out ..."Please tell Becky that I love her and tell them both that I will try to change their suffering."Then Jim faded away to find his way back to the past.

CHAPTER 19

As soon as Jim recovered from the trip, he began to tell the Doc everything his son had told him in the year 2029. The good news was that the Doc's son, Mandy and Becky were alive and well. The bad news was that Jim and the Doc were dead plus the country was in a state of failing Communism or Socialism. Jim wrote down as much of the detail that he could remember and wondered out loud, "What are we going to do about the bleak future?"

One of the reasons that Jim and the Doc were killed in the future was the work with the NSA, so Jim suggested that they somehow get all of the information to agent Jones as soon as possible. He discussed ideas with the Doc about what to tell the NSA and thought of two options that might work; one was to tell Jones that someone had come from the year 2029 and the other was to suggest that Jones send someone to 2029 on a fact finding mission of their own. Either way, Jim felt strongly about telling anyone about their underground facility and the Doc also thought that it would not a good idea. The records of the NSA may fall into the wrong hands in the future and no one needed to know about their traveling capability.

Agent Jones was glad to hear from Jim, so he decided to tell the NSA that someone had come to him from 2029, but he did not give a name. He told Jones that he believed the report of the traveler from the future, but suggested that NSA investigate the information for themselves. Jim did not trust anyone in the present government, including the president, Congress, or law enforcement, so he asked if it would be possible to meet with the first President Bush who lived in Houston and get some advice on how to prevent the atrocities of the future. If the information was accepted, then maybe the second President Bush could be called in and more trustworthy conservatives could be involved in decisions about what to do.

Jim suggested to agent Jones, "My influence will not be as great or trustworthy as members of the NSA group and the selected conservatives, so I will act as a consultant rather than the leader of the movement to change the future."

When Jim left the meeting with the NSA in Houston, he called Becky and asked that she invite the Doc and his family over for supper with the intention of briefing them on the situation and to discuss their options. "How can we stop any of the future problems? Let's make a list," Jim suggested. Their list included the main problems that molded the next twenty years:

The president has a Muslim background and relatives. He came from nowhere, has no experience and mysterious supporters. The liberal press helped him get elected.

The Muslim population increases and eventually takes control of the United States. Rights and freedoms are discarded. Education is limited to the Koran.

The liberal president and Congress pass discriminatory laws and take God out of everything.

Depression is brought on by liberal financial decisions, excessive spending, and give-a-way programs, which include bailouts, buyouts, and takeovers by the federal government.

The small group was realizing that there was probably not much that they could do to stop what was to happen, but they decided to form their plan of action anyway:

1A. There is not much we could do about a bad president unless there was something wrong in his background that could be discovered by time travel.

2A. With a secure Internet connection, the little group might be able to publish a blog or newsletter that would help to inform ordinary people about the dangers ahead.

3A. Rally a group of Christians and patriotic people that want to save the United States and honor God.

4A. Reveal to the voting public where the federal government is heading and what will happen. Help the NSA in everyway possible to redirect the financial future.

"We can encourage the people to ask for God's help and we can pray for the rapture of the church before it gets too bad," suggested Mandy.

CHAPTER 20

During the next three years, the little group that they called the *Truth Team* became involved in publishing a newsletter that was distributed over the Internet. A loyal following of Christians and conservatives forwarded the information to others until the *Truth Newsletter* reached millions around the world. The Muslims and the liberals that did not want this information made public were searching for the infidels and rebels responsible. Their secret organization and untraceable newsletter began to become effective in rallying an underground movement.

The NSA did not regularly keep Jim informed of actions taken, but he could go to the Houston office and read the files or talk to Agent Jones privately. One thing that Jim suggested was a way to get the president impeached by proving that he was not born in the United States. After several trips back to the time of his birth, the president was removed from office over the protests of liberals, Muslims and enemies of the country. The vice president was just as liberal, but he at least was a loyal American and not a Muslim sympathizer.

Jim decided to put the farm and surrounding land in the name of Bill Hopper Jr. because of the possible future invasion of the farm by troops or terrorists looking for him. Either way Bill Jr. could be part of the Truth Team when he was older or it might be necessary for him to farm the land to survive. Some escape routes and contingency plans were made for the Gray family and the Hopper family. Beside the underground chambers for the time travel equipment, they installed and stocked some bomb shelters, for want of a better name, to give them places to hide in case of an emergency.

The NSA did its part to rally the former Bush administration by doing demonstrations of time travel and sharing reports of what was found on their trips to 2029. Jim's name was kept out of the discussion as he had requested and Agent Jones gave him face-to-face reports so there would be no record of their conversations. The conservative coalition managed to thwart some of the give-a-way programs, excessive government spending, and the spread of the Muslims influence by defeating liberal legislation at every occasion.

The *Truth Team* often met for prayer and discussions about their progress, but they also wondered if they were being effective in changing the future. At one of these meetings, the Doc asked if he could go into the future to evaluate their efforts and to see his boy at age twenty-six years old. It seemed like a good idea, so the team began to train for the Doc's trip to 2029. Mandy was apprehensive about her husband going through the spirit removal process, but this time she and Becky would be part of the preparations and travel monitoring.

It took more than a month because the Doc had never traveled and Jim had never operated the equipment without a trained team. Also Mandy and Becky had not been allowed to participate before and now they would be part of the Time Shift operation. When all were ready to do their part, the Doc's spirit was liberated and appeared in the chamber. With a little gesture, he disappeared and Mandy gasped, "He's gone." The Doc willed his spirit to a time and place that was little later on the same day that Jim had visited. That way, Bill Jr. would still be in the barn and the rest of the family would not be encountered. The Doc said, "Son, it's me, your dad."

Bill Jr. was more excited about seeing his dad than he had been only a few minutes earlier when Jim had appeared to him. The Doc said, "I just left your mom and the Gray's back in 2012 and as you know, I only have a couple of hours to visit." "Bill," the Doc said, "I am here to see if anything has changed since Jim's visit. You may not know that it was changed, so just tell me what has happened to our country and the people in the last few years," his dad asked.

Bill Jr. admitted that he had some mixed up memories, but that the president elected in 2008 had been impeached and the conservative groups had been successful in stopping some bad legislation. The vice president from the 2008 election had been reelected by a close majority and the conservatives have gained more seats in Congress.

The Doc asked about the Muslim population and their influence in the country, and Bill Jr. replied, "They have caused problems in the big cities, but many of them have been killed and exported during what amounted to a holy war that took place about six years ago." "A resistance to the liberal government, Muslims, and legislation that takes away the rights of the people came out of a movement started by *The Truth Newsletter* and loyal government agencies on the side of freedom."

The Doc had a great time visiting with his grown son and was thankful to hear that the future was brighter for God's people. It was time to go, so the Doc headed back to 2012 to report the wonderful news. Jim, Becky, Mandy, Doc, and Bill Jr. celebrated when they heard the news from the future. They all agreed that Bill Jr. would be a full member of the *Truth Team.* Of course, Bill Jr. wanted to know, "Who am I going to marry?"

Dr. H. A. Ironside stated in one of his books that the believer may truthfully use the solemnly precious words of Dr. Bonar, as his own:

I murmur not that now a stranger

I pass along the smiling earth;

I know the snare, I dread the danger,

I hate the haunts, I shun the mirth.

My hopes are passing upward, onward,

And with my hopes my heart has gone;

Mine eye is turning skyward, sunward,

Where glory lightens round yon throne.

My spirit seeks its dwelling yonder;

And faith fore dates the joyful day,

When these old skies shall cease to sunder
The one dear love-linked family.
To light, unchanging and eternal,
From mists that sadden this bleak waste,
To scenes that smile, forever vernal
From winter's blackening leaf I haste.
Earth, what a sorrow lies before thee!
None like it in the shadowy past;
The sharpest throe that ever tore the,—
Even though the briefest and the last.
I see the fair moon veil her luster,
I see the sackcloth of the sun;
The shrouding of each starry cluster,
The three-fold woe of earth begun.
I see the shadow of its sunset;
And wrapt in these the Avenger's form;
I see the Armageddon-onset;
But I shall be above the storm.
There comes the moaning and the sighing,
There comes the hot tear's heavy fall,
The thousand agonies of dying;
But I shall be beyond them all."

EPILOGUE

What began as a personal quest to prevent the death of his only son, Jim Gray used the Time Shift technology to help others and eventually the world by traveling through time.

The United States and the rest of the world were headed for disaster which would be led by liberal polities backed by ideologies foreign to the Constitution of the United States. When citizens recognize that the government is moving in the wrong direction, they must use every resource at their disposal to redirect the "Government of the People, by the People" or the Republic will disappear from this earth. Jim Gray helped a few people with technology and saved millions of people from death and loss of freedom. Jim is too old to continue the strenuous activities, but has provided the equipment and the knowledge to others that are ready to move through time and space if it becomes necessary again.

listen|imagine|view|experience

AUDIO BOOK DOWNLOAD INCLUDED WITH THIS BOOK!

In your hands you hold a complete digital entertainment package. Besides purchasing the paper version of this book, this book includes a free download of the audio version of this book. Simply use the code listed below when visiting our website. Once downloaded to your computer, you can listen to the book through your computer's speakers, burn it to an audio CD or save the file to your portable music device (such as Apple's popular iPod) and listen on the go!

How to get your free audio book digital download:

1. Visit www.tatepublishing.com and click on the e|LIVE logo on the home page.
2. Enter the following coupon code:
   fa76-b719-dde9-0857-506a-6eca-f9b8-c118
3. Download the audio book from your e|LIVE digital locker and begin enjoying your new digital entertainment package today!